The Bushido Way

A Sam Phillips Mystery

By

M. Anthony Phillips

The Bushido Way: A Sam Phillips Mystery
M. Anthony Phillips
Bushido954@hotmail.com
314-378-7095
Genre: Crime Novel
Word Count: 69,267

This book is dedicated to my father Sam Phillips—a P.I. Rest in peace.

Acknowledgement to the great crime novelist Elmore Leonard. Rest in peace.

Part One   Soul Power

Los Angeles, circa 1976

Chapter 1

They said I'm not the sharpest tool in the shed. Choosing to become a P.I. was not what my mother had in mind for me after I got out of 'Nam. She wanted me to go into the airline industry, or maybe work for a bottling company. It's 1976— our country's bicentennial year, as most of the country is doing their part to celebrate. I returned in "country" after the fall of Saigon last year with my body intact, but my mind somewhat damaged. Nightmares are a recurring theme, so working in a "normal environment" just doesn't work for me.

I settled in Hollywood, California, by way of Kansas City, Missouri, just to get out of my folks' hair. I took up being a private dick because it was an easy transition from being in the military.

I reside in a dive of an apartment upstairs from a bar that also doubles as my office. It has a pull out sofa for my bed. It's located on Hollywood and Vine, a block away from Capitol Records Music in an area that's a far cry from the glamour of Hollywood's "golden years".

The bar sits around the corner from 24hr strip clubs, porn stores, and tourist shops, and is run by a tough broad by the name of Bernice Jones. Miss Bernice—as she's called was a former blues singer back in the Chess Record days but fell on hard times herself. Underneath the bar she packs a sawed-off shotgun to ward off the riff-raff that either can't hold their liquor or don't want to leave when she tells them. I on the other hand, am the latest to draw Bernice's ire. For what you ask? My rent is due and I can't make rent.

Just yesterday I got a visit from Bernice. She doesn't like to come looking for you on rent day because it takes her away from her other duties. She came in and bowled right over my secretary—Constance Turner. "Where's Sam?!" she asked.

"I think he's out…"

"No, he's not—I can smell his cheap Hai Karate cologne, baby!" Bernice said, storming past Constance. She steps into my office with a look on her face that can scare Aunt Esther. "Sam, you know I don't like coming to find you on rent day!" she yelled. "You should be man enough to come to me even if you ain't got it!"

What can I say—she's right. Only a bum would hide away in his office. "You're right, Miss Bernice. I got caught up calling back potential clients—trying to get a case," I said, even though it's bullshit. I was looking through the paper for the lottery results—loser again. "I'm revoking your drinking privileges at the bar until your rent's paid," she barked. She looks over at my tiny little Fern sitting in the corner that's seen better days. That just happens to be the same Fern that she gave me when I first moved in. Just when she was starting to warm up to me—I can see the veins in her forehead starting to pop.

"You make sure you have my rent by next week, or you're out on your ass!" She moves out of the room exactly the way she came in. Like an F4 Tornado.

Chapter 2

Being cut off from drinking privileges just makes me want to drink even more, but I've got things to do. Bernice means business, but she'll be lucky to get the rent this week. Looking out my window there's a ton of cases out there yet to be solved. I just need to compete with all the grizzled veterans—can you dig it? I need to get out and clear my head—look at things from another perspective. Maybe I'll go and see my old army buddy Joey, down at the precinct. He's an Italian American that helped me get through that damn war. Hell—I helped him also.

I walk up to the front office to see Constance looking at the horoscopes again. She thinks every day that the stars will bring Mister Right walking through the door. Constance is a smart young black woman with a B.A. in business, who hides her looks behind Librarian style glasses and frumpy dresses.

She's been with me since day one, and is the kind of person that sees life half full.

"Any calls Connie?" I asked, looking for any morsel I can get. Constance shakes her head with that angelic smile of hers.

"Nothing so far, boss—it's still early though. I bet you when you come back, things will turn around." Sometimes Constance can be "Stepford Wife" material sometimes with that smile of hers.

"You enjoy your lunch out there, boss—it's a beautiful day out there, isn't it?"

"Yes it is, Connie," I answered back. Connie holds down the fort while I step out to clear my head and get some perspective. I step onto Hollywood Boulevard to get some gossip from newsstand owner Manny, who always has the latest. "What's up Sammy? Taking a break from the rat race?!" Manny asked.

"Manny, what's new?"

"Inflation, Sammy. Everything is up, Gas and Housing. Hopefully Jimmy Carter will kick Ford's butt in November." Manny is a Latino brother who worked hard to get his citizenship, and is now prospering with 2 newsstands.

Manny rambles on about the politics of the day, but my mind is wandering about bigger issues. I need a case so bad I can taste it. Bernice is not going to stand for it much longer. I can only get by on my good looks for so long.

Maybe I'll take a ride over to Pink's for a hot dog—damn I forgot to bring my car! "Hey, amigo—did you hear me?" Manny asked.

"Sorry, Manny, I was day dreaming," I said.

"I asked are you on a new case?" All I can think about at the moment is a Pink's hot dog—now that it's in my head.

"No Manny. I'm in between cases. I need a hotdog from Pink's but I forgot my car."

"No problem, Sam. Take my car." Manny throws me his keys to his Ford Pinto parked in front. It's a dull looking beige color with a few dings here and there. "Bring me one too fully loaded with extra chili peppers," Manny said.

"You got it, amigo."

Chapter 3

I turn the key in the ignition but the car doesn't fire up.
"There's an ignition switch under the dashboard," Manny
said. "It'll stop thieves from getting my car." I smile at
Manny to keep from splitting a gut from laughter. I finally
get the car going and head off to Pink's. As I drive down
Hollywood Boulevard, I start to think about the days spent
with my father as a kid—going on some of his stakeouts.
Those were the times we really bonded. He always told me
don't get too emotionally involved in a case, you'll last
longer. He was an avid reader on a multitude of subjects, but
mainly loved his detective stories. He said they were the
reasons he got into the business, and he became the best at it.

I make it to Pink's and stand in a long line that's typical here. Sandwiches are named after famous stars whose come from miles around on a daily basis. As I'm driving back down La Brea and Hollywood Boulevard, I see all the Bicentennial festivities going on that reminds me of the friends I made back in my unit that didn't make it back alive. I was one of the lucky ones from Charlie Company who made it back in one piece—although the meds I'm taking for recurring nightmares doesn't always work. I make it back to the office after filling my belly, and avoiding Miss Bernice.

"Welcome back, boss," said Constance, with a big smile on her face.

"Connie—what's got you so excited?" I asked. Connie points quietly to my office.

"You have clients in your office," she whispers. It's been a whole month since my last case, so I'll take what I can get, no matter how small the job. I walk back to my office—slash bedroom to find two Asian people—a young lady and man, sitting calmly. They're dressed in nice, fashionable clothes which seem to indicate they're maybe middle class.

"I hope you weren't waiting too long," I said. The young lady smiles at seeing me, which makes me, do a double take. "Sam—you don't remember me do you?" she asked. I stood there with a dumb look on my face—mostly upset when someone remembers me but I don't remember them. That is a big pet-peeve of mine. "I'm sorry…should I?"

"It's me—Michelle! Michelle Yamada!" she said. "My mom used to work for your father. We met years ago just before you went off to war."

"Michelle! Wow—it's been a long time! You were just a skinny little kid from the Valley!" I said. We hug for what seemed an eternity while her brother looks on. "You said you wanted to make a difference…!" We went on for like 15 minutes—reminiscing about the new decade. It was 1970, and Michelle's mom Mariko was my father's secretary. My father always said what a valuable asset she was to him. "This is my little brother, Ken. He went to live with my father in Japan when my parents got divorced," Michelle said. Ken and I shake hands, but I can tell the kid is a man of little words, which mean to me that he's got a whole lot to get off his shoulders.

Chapter 4

Ken is a clean cut looking kid who looks to be around 20
years old who's probably never even had a traffic ticket.
"How is your mom, by the way?" I asked. Michelle's face
suddenly turns sad at the mention of her mother's well-being.
"My mother had a stroke. She's in a nursing home for now,"
Michelle said.

"I'm sorry to hear that. I'll say a prayer." I can tell this
must be very tough on Michelle and Ken. In the Asian
community, it's very rare that senior family members are not
being cared for in the home. "So, how can I help you all
today?" I asked. Michelle pauses for a second to gather her
thoughts as she looks at her little brother. "Our mother told
us that your father owed her a favor and that if she came to
him—he'd be there like she was for him," Michelle said.

"My father was a man of his word, but he's no longer with
us," I said in response.

"You don't assume your father's responsibility after he's gone?" Michelle asked, laying a massive guilt trip on me. Constance walks in and brings me a hot cup of coffee— black, as always. She does it because it's her job, but also to break up the awkwardness. It's something we've worked out together. "Can I get you folks something to drink?" she asked.

"No thank you," Michelle said. Ken shakes his head. Constance gives me the eye and walks back to her desk. "I'd be happy to help your mother out any way I can, but as you can see by my humble surroundings, I can only do so much. I always have people waiting to see me." Michelle smiles, but Ken doesn't get it. I sit back in my chair thinking that the favor maybe about me checking in on her mother, or running occasional errands here and there.

"I'm not sure you're ready for what we're about to tell you, Sam. It's a matter of life and death," Michelle said.

That got my attention—especially if the life or death involves me. "The reason my parents got divorced is because my mother liked the lifestyle of being American, and that my father was the head of the Yakuza in America. When he got called back to Japan, she didn't want to leave what she built for herself here because she felt more independent. In exchange for her freedom, my father insisted on taking Ken with him back to Japan."

"I heard of the Yakuza—that's the Japanese Mafia, right?" I asked. Michelle nods her head. Suddenly, Ken stands up and unbuttons his shirt and sliding it off his arms—letting it fall to the floor to reveal a multitude of outrageous body tattoos covering his whole torso. "That is a lot of tattoos," I said. It's an impressive display of dragons and snakes and other Asian symbols. "I take it that you are a part of this…Yakuza—right, Ken?"

"Yes. For as long as I can remember I have been Yakuza," Ken said proudly.

"Ken and I don't agree on the Yakuza's way of life,"
Michelle suggests. "The Yakuza practically ran Japan with
an iron fist that has hurt Japan's image." Ken has a frown on
his face the way his sister describes his second family.
"Yakuza gets a bad reputation because of all the movies and
news, but we also work with the police to keep the bad
crooks from robbing business owners," Ken snapped.

"You fight the other bad guys because they were fighting
you over protection money that you take yourself!" Blood
will be spilled if I don't separate Michelle and Ken which
will attract the vampire—Miss Bernice.

Chapter 5

Ken begins to put his shirt back on to the disappointment of Constance, whose glasses are fogging up. "You said that the Yakuza ran Japan, Michelle—like they used to. What's changed?" I asked. Michelle takes a deep breath to gather her thoughts as Ken sits back down. "There's a war going on in Japan right now," she said. "The Yakuza is being challenged by a large, young gang bent on taking over the old heads of the…"

"They have no honor!" Ken interrupts. "Their name is the Yokohama Black Rebels. They wear black masks so we can't see their faces. They've killed some of the old bosses by chopping their heads off and delivering them to their men."

"Nice guys," I said. "Okay, you have a gang war going on in Japan—we have gang wars all the time here in Los Angeles, what does that have to do with me?"

For a moment, the room goes quiet like an E.F. Hutton commercial until Michelle finally speaks up. "My brother and father's life is in danger, so my father sent him home here—but my mother is in the hospital. He's getting out of the gang and needs protection."

"My protection," I said.

"Yes," Michelle said, with humbleness.

"If I do this what's to stop Ken from going back to the Yakuza?" I asked, looking right at Ken. What I'm looking for is a sincerity that he wants to get out before I use my resources. "I want to be here for my family," Ken said with his head held high. Michelle places her hand on Ken's in a show of support. She looks at a picture of my father and smiles. "What happened to that fancy car your father owned?" Michelle asked with a smile. I point to the picture of the car with my father standing by it. I remember when he got that car—a gift from a wealthy client for a job well done.

"You mean this car?" I pointed out proudly. A 1965 Buick Riviera Gran Sport—black with maroon bucket seats.

"It's in the parking garage—my father gave it to me in his will." Michelle grabs the picture and looks at it with fondness. "Your father was a great man, Sam," Michelle said, wiping away a tear. I can relate to what she's feeling right now. She's thinking about her mother, and remembering a time when her mother was very happy. "I'll take on your case, Michelle," I said without hesitation. "Unfortunately, business is slow right now—how much can you afford to pay?" A smile appears on Michelle's face along with a sigh of relief from Ken.

"Money is no object—we expected as much," Michelle added. I smile when a client says money is no object. I'm ready to pull out a cigar that I only smoke when I get a new case. "Connie will draw up the papers with you. I'll need $500.00 up front, and $150.00 a day for expenses," I said. We hug and shake hands as I walk them in to see Connie. Returning to my seat, I pull open my desk drawer and pull out a bottle of Cognac and a cigar. I look at a photo of my dad and light up.

Chapter 6

It feels good to be back in the game on a fresh case. The first thing I did was to have Connie pay off Miss Bernice and to have my privileges reinstated—a P.I. has got to have his perks. I follow Ken and Michelle back to their place so he could pack up his belongings to bring back with me. They live in Studio City—an upper middle to high-class area usually frequented by Hollywood celebrities. I drive down Ventura Boulevard in my Riviera, the same car Michelle and I was talking about that gets a few stares from pedestrians and drivers alike. I instruct Ken to sit low in the back seat out of sight.

"What makes you think that these young men will come all the way from Japan to go after you, Ken?" I asked. Ken sticks his head up a moment as he looks out on the streets.

"The Black Rebels are probably already here, Mister Phillips—"

"Call me Sam."

"Sam. The Yakuza are competing with the Triads for control of the Asian businesses—so I'm sure the Black Rebels are already moving in." I lower my window as the temperature starts to reach 90 degrees with a slight breeze—a typical L.A. summer day. "Great, a turf war is being brought here from Asia, huh?" I asked with worry. Michelle turns her head quickly towards me, away from looking outside. "There's a turf war in Little Tokyo, and Chinatown, Sam— you just never hear about it because of the secrecy in the community. We never go to the police for fear of revenge."

"It's Bushido—the Samurai code," said Ken. "It's the Way of the Warrior—to exact revenge without hesitation. No one will talk." I laugh a little because it sounds familiar.

"The Black Community has that same code without all the fancy codes," I said. "It's called don't snitch are you get payback." I laugh, followed by Michelle. Inside their home, I keep an eye out while Ken packs his things. I think about Michelle living alone now that her mother is ill, and the potential for her to come to harm. "And what about you, Michelle—do you have a safe place to stay?" I asked while keeping my eyes looking out the window.

23

"I have a friend I can stay with—no problem," Michelle said with confidence.

"She means…a boyfriend!" Ken said, laughing. I notice a strange looking car outside that I didn't see a moment ago. It could be nothing, but I didn't see anyone get out, so I casually pull out my gun to check to see if it's loaded while Michelle and Ken are busy. "Is everything okay, Sam?" Michelle asked. I wave Michelle over and slightly pull back the curtain.

"Do you recognize that blue Toyota over there?" I asked with suspicion. Michelle takes a hard look and then shakes her head. "No, I don't recognize the car," she replied.

"Stay put while I check it out." I button up my suit coat to conceal my gun holster and walk outside toward the vehicle.

Chapter 7

I walk up to the car occupied by 3 Japanese men trying to look uninterested. Dressed like F.B.I. Agents, I proceed with caution. The driver rolls down his window as its time for me to go into character. "Hi—how ya'll doin'?!" I asked with a southern drawl. The men look at me with disdain. "Ya'll not from around here are ya'?" I asked making sure I see their faces.

"We're looking at house for sale," the driver said, in broken English. I look back at the house next door to Michelle and Ken's place and see the "For Sale" sign. "Oh, that house. I just sold that house to a policeman and his family guys. Here's my card." I pull out one of my many different business cards. It read; Sam Phillips—Real Estate Agent. "I'm introducing a new family to their neighbors," I add. The driver reads the card—crumbles it up and tosses it on the ground. "Say, I paid good money for that card!" I protest.

"I was gonna' ask you to come to the Open House too!" The driver drives off none too happy. I run back to the house to speed up the process. Those guys have already found Ken and Michelle, so they are not amateurs. I may have temporarily fooled them, but they may be back. I go back into the house to find that Michelle and Ken are still not done. For people that want protection that just don't get the message of urgency. "We have to go! Leave the rest—I'll have someone comeback at another time!" I said, stressing the urgency.

"Who was out there?" Ken asked, showing a brave face.

"The bad guys!" I replied. "If they've found you this fast, it means that they have a lot of contacts here. That's going to make my job even harder. I need to break out the big guns." I have Michelle and Ken go out the back where I meet them in the alleyway to throw off the scent of the bloodhounds. Michelle looks back out of the back window to see if they are followed. "What about my car!?" she asked, frantically.

"Don't worry. I'll have someone come back for it," I said. I take Michelle to her boyfriend's place in Woodland Hills—a Los Angeles suburb about 20 miles west of Studio City.

26

She said her boyfriend is a film editor in Hollywood who works on small budget movies like the ones that Roger Corman makes. I watch as Michelle and Ken say their goodbyes to each other while I keep an eye out for any suspicious characters. Ken described to me what to look for with the Black Rebels. They blend in more than the Yakuza because of their refusal of tattoos—just to be different. In Japan, their look is more of an American Black culture that was very funny to me when I heard it. Ken and I make it back to Hollywood as I place a call to my friend, Armstrong Jones, fresh out of the joint for doing six months for beating up three men for foolishly trying to rob him. The judge agreed the beat down by Armstrong was excessive.

Chapter 8

I've been in this business a short time, and on the hard cases I've used Armstrong for his muscle and his ability to get things done. He can be a little unpredictable at times, to say the least, as a couple of times Armstrong thought it would be a good idea to shake down a few clients with scandalous pictures. I've fired and hired Armstrong more times than Steinbrenner's firings of Billy Martin. First thing on the agenda is making sure Ken is secure, so I stash him at the office for now. "Have you had anything to eat, Ken?" I asked. "I could order takeout."

"Can we go out to eat?!" Ken asked, excitedly. "It's been a long time since I've been here." I look at Ken like a man who wants to play Russian roulette with a loaded 357 Magnum. He's crazy. "You're not here on a vacation kid, and I ain't no tour guide," I said calmly, but firm.

I pull two beers out of the mini 'fridge and pass one to Ken as I go over ground rules with Ken. "Tomorrow we go a place I use for situations like this," I said. "It's not the Ritz or the Hilton—it ain't supposed to be. But we'll keep you safe. No phone calls, no opening the door for anyone, and no escaping to go wandering the streets, you got that?"

Ken takes a gulp of the cold beer while I water my fern. "That's a terrible looking plant," Ken said. "Maybe I'm not in good hands if you can't take care of a simple plant."

"Well kid, you got me there. I neglected this little lady, but she's starting to grow on me—no pun intended."

"Japan is full of beautiful flowers and plants," Ken said. I look at Ken as I see the way he's thinking about home. He reminds me of myself sitting in a foxhole with my army buddies. Boy—did I miss home. "Why did you do it, kid?" I asked. "Why did you join the Yakuza?" Ken looks out the window at the Capitol Records building—staring. "My father is the boss. I saw how he commanded respect and fear from his men. Anyone who didn't perform their job or made a big mistake that made the family look bad would commit Yubitsume."

"What does Yubit…sume mean?"

"A soldier would cut off his finger and place it in a towel and place it in front of the boss. He would then apologize for his mistake. The boss could accept the apology or not." I laugh—not because the act is hilarious, but that it's brutal and ritualistic. It's more brutal and final than the Italian mob, unless the mob considered a soldier a liability—then it's a smile, a handshake, followed by two in the back of the head. "So, what if a soldier makes a few mistakes?" I asked.

"There are some soldiers who are missing more than one finger." I look at Ken's fingers and see that he still has all his. It must be good to be the boss' son. "I can see why you would enjoy being in that kind of family," I said with the utmost of sarcasm.

Chapter 9

Ken and me eat Chinese takeout and drink more beer as I find out more about his habits—anything that won't come back to haunt him. Ken explains to me in detail what his tattoos represent, letting me get a perspective of the culture. The Yakuza soldiers are like Samurai working for a Shogun or master. A samurai without a master is called Ronin that means "masterless samurai." I begin to understand the code of honor these men have which goes all the way back to 17th Century.

"Tell me what I'm up against with these…Yokohama Black Rebels," I said.

"For the first time I've seen fear the eyes of my father and other Yakuza bosses," Ken said.

"They are young and fearless, and don't respect honor or the old ways." Ken pauses for a moment as he gathers his thoughts—being a little intoxicated. "In one shootout, they came at us like Kamikazes…yelling YOKOHAMA BLACK REBELS, as they came at us. I've seen a good friend's head rollout in front of me. For the first time, I had wished I was someplace else." After another 15 minutes Ken was out like a light, so I place a blanket over him and go over to my desk to catch up on some paperwork.

The next morning I take Ken to his new home for the time being until this "thing" is over. The place is a small safe house that my father owned in the city off La Brea and Venice Boulevard. I take Ken just early enough that the early birds are just now showering to go to work. Ken looks around the place totally not impressed. There's barely any furniture or odd things to make the place look lived-in. There's a television set, radio, and cards to pass the time away. The window blinds stay shut for obvious reasons.

"It's not the Taj Mahal, but it'll do," I said as I check all the rooms. Ken follows behind me like an inspector with a white glove on. "It looks like your cleaning lady must have quit huh?" he asked, sarcastically.

"What can I say, Ken—inflation is a bitch." Ken sits his bags down in the middle of the room and jumps on the bed still feeling the effects of an all-nighter. "Wake me when breakfast is ready," he said.

"Sure—you have a choice between Mcdonald's or donuts, kid," I said.

"I'll take both." A knock on the door gets my juices going as I pull out my Smith and Wesson, silver .45 caliber pistol with the checkered wood handle and walk to the blinds to look out. After seeing who it was I holster my gun and go to open the door. It's Armstrong. He's looking spiffy in a Nino Cerruti double-breasted suit, Fedora hat, black Stacey Adams, and a white Yves St. Laurent shirt. "I heard you were looking for me," Armstrong said. Armstrong always was a sharp dresser, always trying to one-up me. "Man—get in here!" I replied, pulling him in. I'm definitely happy to see the big guy even though he can be a pain in the ass sometimes.

Chapter 10

Armstrong and I hug each other—playing catch up after his incarceration. "Are you good?!" I asked Armstrong, looking up at his 6'4 inch frame.

"Oh, I'm good my brother—now that I'm outta' the joint. Eating that crappy food made me lose 15 pounds." I punch at his stomach jokingly to test his reflexes like we always do, even though a few months have passed. "Yeah— you're sloppy man!" I said, laughing. "You're terribly out of shape. A couple of sessions with Sifu Wang will take care of that," I added. Sifu Wang has a Kung Fu school 2 doors down from me on Vine Street. Armstrong and I were students there. "How is old Wang doing?" Armstrong asked.

"He asks about you all the time, man—what do you think?" Armstrong smiles and takes a deep breath, obviously happy to be out. "Hey, man—thanks for taking care of my mother," Armstrong said, shaking my hand firmly.

"Hey, you would have done the same thing for me and my mom." Armstrong looks down at my gun in the holster and smiles. "I see you still pack that pee-shooter," he said. I pull out my gun and hold it out proudly making sure the safety is in position. "This is better than your Magnum any day of the week, my friend," I joked back.

I know Armstrong. He mentioned my gun for a reason, and I'll betcha' two courtside seats at the Forum to see the Lakers play that he needs a special favor. "They took my license to carry Sam, is there anyway—"

"I'll make a few phone calls." Ken stumbles out of the room after hearing our conversation. Not hard to do with the thin walls. Armstrong looks at all the tattoos on Ken's body and does a double take. "Man—that had to hurt," he said.

"Armstrong, this is Ken. Ken is Mariko's son," I said.

"Mariko okay?"

"I'll give you the specifics later. Ken was with the Yakuza Japanese Mafia. He needs our help." Armstrong shakes Ken hand with the fervor of a drill sergeant. "This is personal, Armstrong. Mariko is a friend of the family." Armstrong leans in to whisper in my ear just out of earshot of Ken, maybe not knowing that Ken can speak English.

"Does personal mean I don't get paid?" he asked. "It's all good, my brother," I remind him while smiling through my gritting smile. Ken is impressed with Armstrong's size as he looks up at him like David looked up at Goliath. "How did you get so big Mister Armstrong?" Ken asked. Armstrong, who must have heard that question a thousand times, laughs at hearing it from a Japanese person. He must feel like a tourist attraction standing in front of the Hollywood Walk of Fame while the Japanese tourists snap away with their cameras.

"Well, little guy. I make sure I eat from the three food groups; beef, pork, and chicken," he said with a giant laugh. Ken laughs. It's a nice distraction for a moment. "In Japan, you would stand out—be very popular?!"That is a cue for me to hit it and quit. The two of them seem to be hitting it off pretty good. "Well, you two stay cool while I go and get us some breakfast," I said. I pull Armstrong to the side to give him some extra security. I hand him a .38 Special that Armstrong looks at it like its Kryptonite.

"C'mon Sam. You're giving me a .38 man?!"

"See you in 15 minutes."

Chapter 11

I go on a seek and find mission to find breakfast knowing that Armstrong can eat for at least three and a half people— on the day that he's not hungry. Waiting at a traffic light in the Miracle Mile area, I suddenly feel myself being watched and slowly reach for my "peacemaker," until I realized I was being flirted at my three beautiful young ladies—each one just as hot as the other. College girls no doubt, probably attending UCLA up the road.

"That is a hot looking car!" one of the girls said.

"It would look even hotter with three beautiful girls riding in it," I fired back. "You girls I bet, go to UCLA." They all giggle with the two on the passenger side leaning out the window.

"That's right! UCLA Medical School!" they said proudly. Hearing medical school mentioned for a P.I. is like winning the lottery. There is an abundance of cases in the medical field, but I'm no ambulance chaser. Well… "Here's my card, girls. You can call me for business or pleasure," I said with a wink and a smile. The light changes and we went our separate ways.

After dropping off breakfast and explaining to Armstrong the game plan, I head downtown to see my old army buddy Joey at the 2nd Precinct. If there's anyone who can tell me a little about the Asian Gangs, it's Joey. I make it up the precinct stairs just before a summer downpour hits. Joey is a detective in the Asian Gang Unit, along with his partner Tommy Sato.

I check in as usual at the Sergeant's desk. He turns and directs me to the Detective's office. Of course, the first person I see just happens to be the one person who doesn't care for my "friendly visits." Captain Harvey Pierpont has been on the job for 28 years and is retiring in two. He was not a fan of my father who helped with a few cases, but for the most part they butted heads. "It's you again Phillips? Shouldn't you be out finding lost puppies!?" Pierpont asked sternly. "Why yes, Captain. I'm doing that tomorrow.

Thank you." The captain gives me a funny look as always as he continues on his merry way. I come up to the desk of my favorite civilian police officer. Ramona Hightower, a smart and beautiful Black woman, raising a son while also attending night school, checks in all visitors that are here to see the detectives. She's a Pam Grier double, with the body to match. We have an on again, off again relationship for the last two years that gets pretty heavy sometimes. "Ramona— hey baby…"

"Don't hey baby me, Sam Phillips, you stood me up once again," Ramona said, rolling her eyes. I take off my hat and place's it on Ramona's head and bring around one single rose from around my back and place's it in her hand. "I want you to accept my apology, Ramona." Ramona smiles briefly but doesn't want to let me off too easily. "You think a rose is going to change my mind—you don't know me at all." I lean over the desk to whisper in Ramona's ear which makes her giggle from the touch of me up against her neck.

"The Beverly Hills Hilton!?" she asked. "Did you win the lottery?"

"No, but I have a case," I replied back.

Chapter 12

It's on again, as Ramona gives me that familiar smile of hers that can light up Times Square. "Okay, you're back in—for now." And there you have it. What else can a man ask for than a beautiful woman to comfort you on a rainy night? And Ramona fills that need quite well. "You're here to see Joey?" she asked.

"Who's Joey baby? I came to see only you," I said, not being able to convince Ramona otherwise. "Liar." Joey and Tommy Sato come out from an interrogation room, looking spent. Joey slams his fist on his desk in frustration. "That's not a good way to get Workman's Comp, Joey," I said, smiling.

"What's up paison?" Joey replied back, rushing over to greet me. We hug each other, like we always do. It's a constant reminder that we survived 'Nam—well…physically mostly.

40

We always talk about looking up the rest of our unit over a couple of beers, but after we sober up we keep moving on, trying not to look back. It was the great Satchel Paige who said; "Don't look back—something maybe gaining on you." Prophetic words to us vets.

"What's up, Tommy?"

"Sam, what brings you down?" Tommy asked.

"New case, man," I said. Joey nods his head—happy for me. "It's a favor for a family friend." Joey pats me on the back, somehow thinking less of my good fortune. "Pro-bono sucks, man," he said. "It's a legit case Sherlock," I fired back. Joey and Tommy look at each other—laughing under their breath. "I guess you guys have already heard of the war between the Yakuza and the Yokohama Black Rebels," I said, scoring a back-hand slap and bringing them back down to a level we all can deal with. I have their full attention.

"What do you know about that, brother?" Joey asked.

"Let's just say my client is involved all the way up to his neck—if you know what I mean," I said. Joey looks around the precinct as if he's got great information to the whereabouts of Noah's Ark. "We'll show you ours if you show us yours," Joey said.

"I'll bite. What you got?" Joey and Tommy take me to look inside the "box" at a suspect i40

involved in a couple of gruesome killings. He's just a kid— around the same age as Ken, I guess, but with a cold stare looking back at us, even though he can't see us. He shows no fear from the police. "He's a cold-blooded killer," said Tommy. "The Yakuza have been at the top of the food chain—now they've become the hunted."

"Well, he's definitely not Yakuza. No tattoos," Joey points out.

"What do you have on him, Joey?" I asked. Joey finishes off a cigarette and douses it in an ash tray. "Not a damn thing. He just happened to be at a crime scene kind of enjoying the atmosphere a little too enthusiastically."

"Yeah, like an artist standing back and enjoying his masterpiece," Tommy adds. The captain comes back in the room stuffing down a hoagie—dunking it in his coffee. "You still here Phillips?!" he said in his gruff tone. "What you got Detectives?"

"We got squat Captain," Joey said.

"Kick him. I don't need the headache from the Japanese community," Pierpont barked. Tommy cringes at the hoagie and coffee mixing. "How can you do that Captain?" he asked. Pierpont finishes off the hoagie and drinks the rest of the coffee. "This is coming from someone who eats raw fish."

Chapter 13

I can tell Joey, and Tommy are not pleased with the captain's decision, but they understand. The kid covered his tracks, and he knows no one is speaking up in Little Tokyo. The kid laughs at the detectives on his way out the door. "Fuck me!" Joey snapped. "We can use a win in our favor for once!" Tommy suddenly gets pumped, like an old lady winning a round at Bingo. "The captain told us to kick him, but he didn't say we couldn't follow him, partner," he said. Tommy's quick thinking it was just what the doctor ordered with Joey, as he grabs his hat off the coat rack.

"Are you up for a little visit to Little Tokyo Sam?" Joey asked while on the move.

"Do Black folks watch Good Times?" Joey and Tommy laugh because it's obvious—they watch Good Times too.

Back at the safe house, Armstrong is getting Ken associated with American television.

Watching an episode of Soul Train, Ken is up on the floor trying to "bust a move" like the dancers on the show. "Man, you better sit down before you hurt yourself," Armstrong said as he almost cracks a rib from laughter. Armstrong falls out of his seat when Ken tries to do the robot like the Soul Train dancers. "Man, you're killin' me!" Armstrong laughs out loud. Armstrong gets up off the floor as he looks at the show and Ken.

"Kid…the show is called "S-o-u-l Train!" Armstrong said with conviction. "Let me show you how it's done, kid!" Armstrong proceeds to do "the robot," which at his size he must look like Ultra-Man to Ken. The two of them carry on, doing the robot—trying to outdo each other.

As I ride along with Joey, and Tommy, my mind wanders to a place and time I don't care to remember. Joey and I are on patrol in the jungles of Vietnam with the rest of our unit—laughing and joking about nothing particular.

David, a young white kid from Chicago, who volunteered for duty, was going on about his love for the Chicago Cubs. The poor kid falls in a rigged hole filled with sharp-wooden spikes that go through his body. It was the screaming that I can't get out of my mind. It reminded me of a little dog I'd seen get his legs run over by a car. I watched in horror, sitting in my car—the contorted face and scream the little dog did as he crawled to the other side of the street. The sergeant—not wanting the kid to suffer, did what he had to do that none of us grunts had the balls to do. He ended the kid's life with two quick shots to the chest. David was just on his first tour. We didn't have time to say a prayer for him because the Sarge knew that the Gooks heard everything. I pop two capsules in my mouth used for nightmares fully aware that I'm starting to take them more frequently. Joey and Tommy are recognized by the merchants in this tight-knit community as word spreads as fast as a virus in a small town.

Chapter 14

We continue to follow the suspected gang member as he travels on foot through a throng of people. The detectives picked a wrong time to follow someone as this week is full of Japanese festivals. "We'll never keep track of him through this crowd," said Joey.

"Didn't you both get the message that there were festivals all week?" I asked as I look at all the banners—knowing I didn't have a clue myself. It's a colorful display—Japanese and Chinese festivals usually are, loaded with traditional costumes of dragons, samurais, Geishas and more. "We better get out here," Tommy suggested, pulling over to the curb.

Some people in a festive mood run toward us getting in our view of the suspect.

Tommy locates the kid and tap Joey on the shoulder. "He ducked into that Sushi bar!" Tommy said as we weave in and out of the crowd like a running back going through a gauntlet of tacklers.

The sun comes out, leaving a rainbow over the horizon, putting a finally to the rain shower. Tommy is the first to go in, with Joey following, and then me holding up the rear.

We're met inside by a beautiful waitress looking to seat us for lunch. "Hello—three for lunch?" she asked. Joey and Tommy look around for their guy whose nowhere in sight.

"We're looking for the guy who just came in here. We're meeting him for lunch," Joey said. The waitress looks befuddled, acting as if we are her first guests. "No one come in before you, sir. You are first guests in last 15 minutes," she said with confidence.

"Are you sure he came in here, partner?" Joey asked Tommy.

"Positive. This place must be a front for their operation,"
Tommy replied. They've been in enough so-called legit
businesses to smell when there's something illegal going on.
Joey eyes the Sushi chef, and iron chef who's giving the
detective's the evil eye. "What the fuck are you looking at?!"
Joey asked sternly, not liking the smirk on the sushi chef's
face. "You know the man that just came in here?"
The sushi maker keeps wrapping sushi, ignoring Joey.
"Tommy," Joey snarled. Tommy speaks to the man in
Japanese—asking him the same question, and getting the
same response. Joey, not liking the disrespect they get from
the community tries to go around the counter at the man but
is held back by Tommy. "You fucking cocksucker! You
know something," Joey said. "Easy, partner," said Tommy.

"We could lose our badges here." Suddenly we're met by
several young men from the back that are not coming out to
give us a hearty greeting. To say that these guys are spooky
is an understatement. "Detectives, this is a respectable
restaurant," one of the men said, who looks like he's in his
fifties, much older than the rest. "We don't want any
trouble."

The young kid who we followed here is not with these guys. "Who are these guys?" Joey asked the man. "They're my business associates—visiting from Japan. Their English is not as good as mine," the man joked. A stare down ensues for what seemed like an eternity until Joey finally realizes he has to know when to pick his battles. "Let's go partner," Tommy said, dragging Joey out.

"You guys better keep your noses clean while you're here in town you got that?!" Joey said.

As we walk out I got the feeling that someone was watching us. I believe Tommy was right about that kid being there, but of course, we couldn't prove it. A serious looking man comes from around the back of the restaurant standing next to the suspect. All the men and ladies bow at him in a show of respect.

Chapter 15

I make it back to the "safe house" with a vulnerable feeling that there's more to learn about the Yokohama Black Rebels. There secrecy will have to be approached from a different angle than I'm used to tackling. I need someone in L.A who has their pulse into what's happening in the community of Little Tokyo. I need someone who can fit in and spy for me. I obviously can't use Ken because the gang is looking for him. I take over for Armstrong, who seems to have taken to Ken more than I expected. He's even taught Ken a soul handshake before he departs.

"See you later—Little Brother," he said to Ken. Ken holds up a peace sign in solidarity.

"Catch you later…Brother." As I try not to laugh out loud, I walk Armstrong to the door to see him out. "Little Brother?" I asked Armstrong.

"The little dude's okay, man," Armstrong responded. "He just loves the Black Experience—can you dig it?"

"Yeah, I can dig it. Don't get too close my brother, because we don't know how this will all turnout. I need your head clear and focused. These are some serious and crafty cats we're dealing with." Armstrong takes off promising to return later tonight—giving me some quality time to pick Ken's brain some more. "It seems like you and Armstrong are getting along just fine, Ken," I said. Ken takes out a pack of Cool's and lights up one—blowing several rings in the air. I could never do that before I kicked the habit.

"He's cool. I like him," Ken said. "He said he wants to open his agency someday."

"Oh, he did huh?" I asked. "He never told me that." Ken is feeling pretty full of himself—not in a bad way, but now that he has his "Black Card," he's "In like Flint."

"Oh, yeah—we're like that," he went on—holding his two right fingers crossed over. "It's a stone gas, man. We're two brothers from…the same mother."

"I think you mean two brothers from another—never mind." All I can do is laugh. What the hell. The kid is funny. I can see why Armstrong took to him.

"Hey, what do you want for lunch Ken?" I asked.

"Can we go out?!" Ken asked, like a kid wanting to go out and play baseball with his friends. My gut reaction was to say no, but I didn't want to bring the kid's high down. "Sure we can. I know someone that owns their own restaurant. Trust me—the Rebels will never think to look for you there," I said with confidence. "First we'll have to get you some dark glasses and a cool baseball cap."

We head south—deep in the Black Community to introduce Ken to his kin folks. "Welcome to Long Beach, Little Brother," I said. Ken momentarily takes off his sunglasses to get a real look at the Black Experience.

Chapter 16

Ken is brought back into reality with a different take on
urban life than watching Soul Train. It's a hard thing to face
from someone who grew up in an exotic country. The Black
Rebels wouldn't be caught dead on this part of town because
they would stand out like Blacks at a Klu Klux Klan rally.
"Where are we going?" Ken asked cautiously. I laugh to
myself because the swagger is no longer a part of Ken's
vocabulary.

"I'm taking you for some Soul Food, my friend," I said.
"Now that you're an honorary Soul Brother you have to
acquire a taste for our food."

"What kind of food is it?"

"Don't worry—you'll love it," I said. "Just don't ask
what's in the food," I joked.

I take Ken to see my mom—Delores, who owns the restaurant—Momma Dee's Just Like Home Cooking. It was a labor of love for my mother. After working as a lab technician for 30 years in Missouri, she was able to put away enough money to follow her dream and open her first restaurant. This location is her second opening—the other is at home. I know she opened this one to keep an eye on me.

We pull up in the restaurant's big parking lot that has a Grand Opening sign on the building. "Have you eaten here yet?" Ken asked.

"That's a dumb question kid. My mom owns the place." We walk inside the place to a packed house of hungry patrons with some people standing—waiting for service. "Wow—this place is very crowded!" Ken said. Ken tries to look at the menu board as the southern aroma permeates throughout the restaurant. "C'mon Ken—I want you to meet someone," I said, dragging him to where all the action takes place.

"Hello Momma." My mother—all 5'5 inches of a ball of fire of her, head my way as I open my arms. She promptly comes over and smacks me across the face—not hard, but enough to get my attention. "Where were you for the grand opening yesterday?!" she asked. A shocked Ken turns his head away from the embarrassment. "I'm on a new case, Momma!" I replied back to the amusement of the staff. In Ken's world, I should be offering up my finger about now, but I'm not going there. I try to get a quick taste of some baked, homemade macaroni, but she smacks my hand away like she did when I was a child. "You know I would have been here if I could," I said, eying the smothered pork chops and mashed potatoes with gravy. "Are you going to give your favorite son and his friend a lunch plate or am I going to have to go hungry for the day?" I asked. "Don't con me boy," she said. My mother looks at Ken and begins to change her mind.

"What's your name, baby?"

"Ken Yamada."

"You're from Japan, huh?" Mom asked. Ken nods his head.

"You—I'll give a taste." Mom pulls a small plate and proceeds to spoon a nice portion of macaroni, and a slice of meatloaf—the smell almost knocking Ken down. Ken tastes a spoonful that causes his taste buds to explode.

"This is very good!" he said while plunging his fork deeper into the macaroni as I standby useless. "Since you've got a new case you can afford to buy your lunch," my mother said.

Chapter 17

Momma Dee's has shut down after lunch to get ready for the dinner crowd. My mother and I take time to catch up over a cup of coffee and sweet potato pie. Ken is enjoying all the comforts of a Southern meal which is evident in his expanded waistline. "Did you get enough to eat, baby?" Momma asked. Ken, still chewing the last of the pie nods his head in approval. "He'll never go back to sushi," I joked. Momma laughs because she's seen a lot of converts.

"When are you going to quit that job of yours and join me in the family business?" Momma asked. My mother and I don't see eye to eye on my career choice. She's seen firsthand how my father struggled to keep his business afloat. But he persevered and became one of the best P.I's ever.

"Momma—this is "the" family business—on Dad's side. I'm
happy that you've found something that makes you happy. I
never tried to discourage you from following your dream of
opening a restaurant. Most restaurants fail in the first year.
What I'm doing is all I know. And I'm good at it." After a
few more rounds at it, we finally come to an agreement. We
hug and kiss, and of course, she did send us off with a hot
plate of the best soul food in town.

I dropped Ken off at the safe house with Armstrong with
an additional plate of food, knowing the big guy would kill
for a plate of Momma's cooking. It's time for my rendezvous
with Ramona, and this time I'm not going to stand her up.

After picking up some flowers and a bottle of wine, I pick
up Ramona in Culver City and when I get to her place I'm
blown away by her looks. Wearing a form-fitting, white Sun-
dress, I must have forgotten how "ample" she is. "Well,
Officer, I must say you've managed to raise my blood
pressure in all the right places," I said. There's a slight breeze
that blows Ramona's hair and dress gently—like a model,
running on a white sandy beach.

"You don't look so bad yourself, Mr. Phillips," Ramona said. She kisses me for the flowers as we turn onto Wilshire Boulevard on our way to the hotel. I made sure to have the hotel have the room prepared with everything I requested on our arrival. As we head up to our room on the elevator, we get a snobby look from a Beverly Hills couple who obviously don't think we belong there. Ramona's expression tells it all, as her self-esteem is lowered—for the moment, as I grab her in front of those snobs and lays "one" heavy on the lips that must have lasted a millennium—just enough to make those plastic surgery rejects squirm. Ramona has her spirit lifted as we laugh when that couple gets off at the next floor.

When we get back to the room and open the door to walk in Ramona's jaw "drops to the floor" in amazement. The room is littered with balloons, red rose pedals and a nice spread to compliment her big day. It's her birthday. She jumps in my arms and gives me a big one too. "You remembered!" she said. I could swear I could feel her heart beat which gives me a warm feeling inside. Hell—the lady deserves it, putting up with a hard-ass like me. We make love all night long with Ramona reaching a few octaves, like a buxom opera singer.

Chapter 18

After recovering from an incredible night, I relieved
Armstrong the next morning to play babysitter to Ken for the
day. I inform Ken that the police would like him to come
down and look at some pictures, which took a lot of
convincing on my part. I make sure to keep Ken in the
backseat with his hat over his eyes because we're heading
downtown. "Keep low, Ken. And when we get to the station,
we're going in the back entrance, you got it?" I asked.

"I got it, boss," he replied casually. "I was a part of the
Yakuza society. We know how to be discreet." The kid was
right; I guess. The Yakuza have been around as long as this
country was a Union. We make it inside the station, and I
receive a different greeting from Ramona than the other day.

A smile greets me as wide as the Grand Canyon as Ramona is still looking fine—with her afro looking as fresh and tight as always. She knows we don't have time for chit-chat, so we remain professional.

"The detectives are expecting you Sam—go right in," she said. As I look back, I get a wink and a hand jester for me to call her. I give her a reassuring smile and leave it at that. Ken gets a few weird stares from some L.A.'s finest as we walk by, thinking he was a suspect. I get that same evil look from Captain Pierpont I always get, but this time he's looking at me from the confines of his office as he's getting an earful from the mayor about the rash of killings in Little Tokyo. He stands up and closes the door while listening like a sub-servant lackey.

"Come in Sam," Joey said as they hold the door open to the interrogation room. The interrogation "the box" as some call it, is a very cold and a manipulative place that has broken a lot of strong-minded people. Sometimes it gets so heated up in there that I have thoughts of the North Vietnamese interrogating and torturing soldiers. Thankfully, I was never a P.O.W. "Is this your boy, Sam?" Joey asked.

"No—he's my client, Joey," I corrected him. Joey's destroying a whole pack of gum while staring at Ken. I hope he's not looking to work Ken over. Tommy asks Ken his name in Japanese. "Ken Yamada," Ken responds. Ken and I sit down—me acting like some type of lawyer sitting next to his client to make sure the detectives don't ask the wrong question. Tommy offers Ken a cigarette which Ken eagerly except. "I'm Detective Sato—my partner's name is Detective Sorvino," Tommy said. Tommy places a large book of photos in front of Ken of notorious Japanese gangsters. "What can you tell us about this new gang that's taking over the Japanese community," Tommy said. Ken looks through the pictures and for the most part he just sees Yakuza.

"It started about ten years ago when Boss Watanabe had his closest rival, Boss Ito and his family wiped out—except for his son—Hiroshi, who escaped. Hiroshi promised revenge by using the old ways of Bushido. He killed Boss Watanabe and fled to Yokohama. There, he started the Black Rebels.

The soldiers dress in black masks that represent different ranks, whereas the assassins can dress like a regular businessman. The assassins only kill high-level rivals—the bosses, and sometimes their whole family."

"Pretty organized aren't they?" Joey asked. Ken finishes looking through the book.

"Those are mostly Yakuza soldiers. I recognize some of them—they're dead now. The other photos can be them, but they could also be regular businessmen. Detective Anderson rushes in with hot news that breaks up the conversation. "Joey, there's another murder! It's at a Japanese steam bath house," he said.

"Let's go Tommy!"

"You mind if I tag along Joey?" I asked.

"What about your client?" Joey asked, hurried. He's right. I forgot about Ken in the rush of the moment. "I'll be alright here," Ken said.

"You sure, Kid?"

"I can keep that foxy momma out there company."

"Keep your hands to yourself—she's got a gun. I'll see you in 20 minutes," I said on the way out.

Chapter 19

It was like a ghost town in Little Tokyo when we arrived today. Terrified, the store owners remain inside their businesses as the Crime Scene Unit go over the murder scene in detail. The yellow tapes block off the street as we arrive. The bath house is owned by the Yakuza—the Mosimoto Clan. Spent shells on the ground outside seem to indicate shots exchanged as the murderers fled. It's an intense scene as the detectives, and I enter the bath house with gang members—still dressed with only their towel, are all over the place.

"Man, what a bloodbath," Joey said, looking at the blood splattered bodies. "Three men and two women are dead, including Boss Mosimoto himself—shot twice in the chest, and once in the forehead. His cigar is still dangling from his mouth. "Partner—get ready for a big body count," Tommy said. "That's Mosimoto lying there.

He was the biggest fish in the pond." Joey gets upset over the killing of the two girls as their bodies are dragged out of the whirlpool. "Where's the fucking respect, man! The Mafia would never kill the civilians!" he barks while looking at the Mosimoto Gang.

"That was the old Mafia, Joey. The days of Lucky Luciano and Meyer Lansky are gone. Drugs are involved—all bets are off." Joey walks over to the gang members who try to keep a stiff upper lip throughout the ordeal. Five menacing looking soldiers stand around looking innocent, when in reality they're probably plotting their revenge.

"Anyone see anything?" Joey asked, knowing he's exercising in futility. No one speaks up.

"Joey—there's a trail of blood leading out the front door," I said.

"Someone's wounded bad. He won't get far with that blood loss," Tommy observed. Joey waves over one of the police officers. "Radio into the station to check with the local hospitals for Asian gunshot victims," Joey said. The officer radios in while Joey and Tommy put two and two together. They draw their guns and order the men on the floor.

"GET DOWN ON THE GROUND—NOW!!" they shout. I pull my weapon and back the guys up.

"Where's the guns?!" they ask, sternly. An officer finds two Mac 10's underneath towels.

"We found something Detectives!" he shouts. Joey and Tommy look over at the guns. Holes in the walls confirm a fierce gun battle. "I'm willing to bet those guns are not registered, partner!" Joey said, smiling. "You guys are going done for a weapons charge unless you play ball," he added. Tommy repeats what Joey said in Japanese. Joey and Tommy cuff the men along with a police officer. "You have the right to remain silent—what you say can and will be used against you…" Tommy states on, as the men are stood up and taken out.

I realize while what's remaining of the Mosimoto Clan is being herded out, is that the killings are escalating and that it was a mistake on my part to leave Ken alone.

Part Two The Streets Run Red

Chapter 20

As we make it back to the precinct, I know I have to do something quick to avoid trouble with Ken and the Mosimoto Clan. "Joey—I need to get my client out of the office first. Give me time to get him out the back," I said.

"You got it, Sammy," Joey said. I take off ahead of the guys to a smiling Ramona, who's playing host to a well attentive Ken. "Welcome back, Sam," Ramona said.

"I'll talk to you later, baby!" I said as I grab Ken by the arm. "Let's go, kid!" We escape out the back just as the detectives bring their suspects in. With each passing moment, the intensity is starting to rise, prompting me to crave a cigarette. Sure, a victory cigar is one thing, but I was able to keep that in control. My vices have gotten me into trouble—especially my gambling and drinking—a deadly mix if you're also taking prescription meds. Man—I need a drink.

"Why did we leave in such a hurry Sam?" Ken asked.

"The truth—I didn't want you getting spotted by the Mosimoto boys," I said. "I don't know who to trust—so I trust no one." Ken pulls out a fresh pack of Cool's and begins to unravel the wrapper as if to taunt me. He lights up a cig' and puffs on it similar to the way I did in the jungle. The aroma is calling me like a 5 dollar whore. Instead—I pull out a Blow pop and tear into the wrapper to keep my mind off the smell.

I've driven at least 2 miles now heading West on Venice Boulevard when I noticed the same brown Buick Skylark tailing us. "I almost had that secretary's phone number," Ken said, oblivious to what's happening. I put my blinker on to move towards the inside lane of the street. Just like I thought—they make the same move. "Kid, get down on the floor—this could get ugly," I said, looking out my rear view mirror. Ken instinctively looks around first to see what it is. "Get down!" I demanded. I take off like a bat out of hell—flying past a just turned red light as horns sound off with the Skylark in close pursuit. "What's happening?" Ken shouts out.

I pull out my gun to get ready for the onslaught, with my head spinning in all directions. "It's the Black Rebels I presume. The bastards must have staked out the bathhouse and followed us to the precinct. It's a smart move on their part!"

"I told you! You can't underestimate them!" Ken said, trying hard not to be thrown from one side of the car to the other. I weave in and out of traffic—being thankful I'm not on the 405 Freeway. "What the hell are they packing in that Skylark? I can't shake'em." The Skylark speeds up and moves on the side of me. Suddenly I see an arm reach out the passenger window with a MAC 10 and open fire. I feel a sharp pain in my left arm as I pull back to avoid further shots.

"I've been hit!" I shout, which pisses me off more than anything else. I made it through 'Nam just to go through this shit, I thought to myself. I race around from the back onto the driver side and unload a full clip of my .45 into their car, causing the driver to lose control of the vehicle—flipping the car over and over. The car finally comes to a stop as fire begins to start up.

The car has at least three occupants that I can see with the driver moaning from being shot. I pull the little runt out of the car just as the heat and flames intensify. Screaming at me in Japanese I knock him out with one punch to the jaw just as the car explodes. Ken looks on, realizing that he's not in Kansas anymore.

Chapter 21

I called Armstrong to come quick to grab Ken and take him
away before the police arrive. The station filled with
Japanese Yakuza and Black Rebels, and having my client
mixed up in that climate ain't cool. Armstrong arrives in his
gold and black Deuce and a Quarter—except for my Riviera,
it's the baddest car Buick ever made.

"What's up Sam!?" he asked with urgency. "Get Ken out
of here quick, Armstrong!" I said as the faint sound of police
sirens saturate in the background.

"Who's this?" Armstrong asked while pulling on a
surprisingly calm Ken.

"He's a Yokohama Black Rebel. He tried to kill Ken and
me."

"You little…Mother Fucker…!" Armstrong angrily said,
while wrapping his big hand around the gang member's
throat.

"Oh, you're gonna' kill him right in front of me and these people forming out here, brotha'?!" I asked sarcastically. "Get out of here, man! I'll catch up later." Armstrong releases the frightened gangster who tried to put up a brave front—which is hard to do when your eyes are bulging out of your head. Armstrong takes my advice and leaves the scene like he stole something, leaving skid marks along the way.

LA's finest arrive and wouldn't you know it—Captain Pierpont arrives with his driver and several police cruisers. The captain struts over like the cock of the walk—spitting and chewing gum like it's going out of style, and barking orders like he's George S. Patton. I hold onto the de-fanged gangster while Pierpont heads my way. "Relax kid—you're going to be famous," I said.

"It's you again Phillips?!" Pierpont shouted. He's obviously not happy to see me. "What the hell do you have to do with this? Don't tell me—it'll only give me a fucking headache." The crime scene tape is placed down while the captain tears me a new one. "This guy and his friends over there—what's left of them tried to kill me Captain. They followed me from the police station, and I took off after they fired shots at me…"

"Causing panic in the streets?!" Captain Pierpont protests.

"Would you rather that it's me over there in the burning car, Captain?" Pierpont raises those bushy eyebrows of his. "Don't tease me, Phillips. You're not a cute little Asian girl, and I'm not a young stud like I used to be. All I have is the little Mrs. at home waiting for me with a hot water bottle and a glass of Bourbon to soothe my aching bones."

"You too, huh Captain?" I asked sarcastically. Pierpont gets in my face smoking a cigarette—knowing I can definitely use one about now. "I'm going to ask you straight Phillips, and you better get it right, or you're going downtown in cuffs. Why were these hoodlums trying to kill you?" I look down on the captain, and then look away.

You never look give a rabid bulldog eye contact. "My professional opinion is that…they are at war with the police and that they thought I was one of you guys."

Pierpont looks me in the eyes and comes to his conclusion.

"Officer, arrest this turkey along with his new friend here. I'm tired of looking at his lying face!" Pierpont shouts. I turn around and assume the position, thinking about my next move. The Yokohama Black Rebels drew first blood. And like James Brown said—this papa's gotta' find his new bag.

Chapter 22

I arrive at the precinct, not by invitation, but as a possible criminal suspect. Of course, it's bullshit. The captain is trying to tell me in his warped way that when it comes to whipping out both our dicks for measurement—he's Superman, and I'm Mickey Mouse. Pierpont is pretty predictable. Next thing that comes out of his mouth is that…he wants my license. "Phillips—your license is dead!" Captain Pierpont said. "You left a train wreck out there with three men dead that are unrecognizable—needless to say what the cost is going to be!"

"Captain, let's be honest with each other. If something had happened to me, you would be crushed," I said. "C'mon, Captain—I was the one being pursued here. I even got you a suspect to interrogate. Don't that count for something? At least take these handcuffs off for Christ sake."

Pierpont gives the nod to an officer who takes the cuffs off.

"I don't like you, Phillips. I don't like what you represent."

"I'm sorry you feel that way, Captain," I said. "I'm just doing the job that you guys don't have time to do. And I always work with you when I can."

"You mean like harboring a potential witness in this case?!" I look across the room and see the Yakuza men staring at us—trying to pick up whatever clues they can. So I lower my voice as not to give away anything that might come back on me. "My client has come in voluntarily and made a statement—full of details about this other gang. Now, I'm not going to say another word unless it's in your office. There are too many eyes and ears around here that can put my client in harm's way." The Yakuza soldiers are taken in separate interrogation rooms and are grilled by the other Asian Gang Unit Detectives. Maria Ozawa, Charlie Thompson, and Fred Washington, help out Joey, and Tommy. Joey and Tommy grill the Black Rebel soldier in an intense setting.

"I want to know what your organization is up to, kid!" Joey asked sternly, grabbing the collar and throat of the gangster. Tommy looks over the black mask which has very distinctive markings on them. "Look at this mask, Joey. See how it's aligned with these weird markings next to each other..." Joey looks at the mask's markings.

"I see it. So what?" he asked.

"These markings represent kills. This mask has five stripes that mean that this kid has five kills to his name," Tommy said. The Black Rebel laughs at the detectives in a taunting manner. "Is he laughing at us?" Tommy asked. The Rebel's taunting enrages Joey, who moves around the table and close lines the kid—knocking him out of his chair. "Now that's funny!" Joey barks. The smile is wiped away from the gangster's face. "You punks come into our town and think you own it. We allow you to be here!" Tommy said in Japanese.

"Yokohama...Black...Rebels will take...over your town," the young gangster said in broken English—mockingly. "You're a bad ass, huh," said Joey.

"Let me tell you something kid, just in case you weren't keeping score. Three of your friends are dead, and we got you dead handed. That means you're going down for attempted murder. You're spending time in an American prison where you're outnumbered twenty to one tough guy." Tommy opens the door to the room letting in Officer Lou Granger.

"Lou, take this piece of shit down for processing," Joey said. Lou takes the Black Rebel gangster out of the room at the same time one of the Yakuza soldier comes out. As they cross paths, the Yakuza gangster grabs the gun from the officer's holster. "GUN!!" Ramona shouts. The Yakuza gangster pumps two bullets into the Black Rebel before the police kill him. Tommy and Joey rush out of the interrogation with guns drawn as I rush out with the captain. Joey and Tommy bend over the dead Black Rebel.

"I guess he pissed off one too many people, partner," Tommy said.

"Save us the paperwork, man."

Chapter 23

After a day of days like this one, it's time to head for my favorite watering hole. Bertha's place is the right cure for what ails me. The gang is all there including Constance, Manny, Joey, and Tommy. Ramona is due to show up any minute now. The place is lively after 5:00P.M, with people getting off work and all, including the people who put their lives on the line.

Jenny is on tonight as bartender. She's a real looker with a stripper's body and an angelic face that would talk a man down from jumping from a ten story building. She's here like everyone else from out of town is doing…working part time while she auditions for acting jobs. Darlene and Jack—a gay man from West Hollywood, are doing the serving.

"Don't worry Sam, she'll get here," Joey said, catching me glancing at my watch. Joey looks hard at Constance for the first time—noticing a slight deviation from her business attire. "Boy, Constance. When you let your hair down, there's a little bit of a Lois Lane—Bat Girl vibe to you," he said.

Constance smiles sheepishly as the effect she was going for is a hit. "Why thank you Joey. I'm glad someone noticed," she said, looking my way.

I have to admit; the little librarian—mousy demeanor has held back a Butterfly. "You do look good, Connie," I said. Constance smiles while taking a sip from her straw of her Coke soda. Ramona finally walks in—stopping at the door first to make sure everyone catches an eyeful. She continues in—strutting to the beat of her own theme music it seems because the lady has a rhythm all to herself.

"What's up everybody?" Whatever confidence Constance had in herself took a major hit as everyone has their eyes fixated on Ramona's curves in her tight skirt. "Hi Constance," Ramona said. "I haven't seen you in a while."

"Hello," Constance replied without looking at Ramona.

"Did I miss anything Suga'?" Ramona asked me, softly. Jack brings Ramona a menu and places it in front of her. "Hello Ramona. I love the dress girl," he said. "Maybe I can borrow it sometime."

"You can borrow it anytime, sweetheart."

"Will there be anything else Detectives?" Jack asked. Joey cringes while Tommy eyes Ramona. "We're good, Jack," I said. Jack walks away to handle other customers. Joey picks over his fries while staring at Jack. "Why does Miss Bernice keep that queer on? He's a buzzkill, man."

"Be easy paisan. Jack's cool," I said.

"You know what I'm sayin', right Sam? No disrespect."

"He's gay, my brotha,' so what. You don't think there was nobody in our unit that was gay."

"No fucking way, man!" I laugh at Joey's ignorance. I signal to Jack to bring me another shot of Tequila. "I say live and let live, you dig?" I said. Tommy must have had a few drinks too many, because he's becoming way too obvious when it becomes to Ramona. "Ramona—when are you going to give us Asian Persuasion's a chance with you?" he asked, prompting a smile from Ramona.

"You never stepped up to the plate, Tommy. Besides, I might be taken off the field soon," she said, looking my way.

Chapter 24

Miss Bernice walks toward our table wearing a smile on her face—which is highly unlike her. Miss Bernice scares people, and she doesn't bring good cheer. "Hello everybody. Are you all having a good time?" she asked.

"Great, Miss Bernice," Constance said, holding up her glass. Everyone else chimes in as well with pleasantries—raising their voices because of the alcohol. "Good…good. Sam—can I see for a moment?" Miss Bernice asked. I wipe my mouth with a napkin—curious as to what the "Iron Lady" wants. "Should I come also, Sam?" Constance asked, almost getting out of her seat.

"Why don't you stay Connie," Joey insisted, showing quite the interest all of a sudden. I can tell from Connie's demeanor that she's uncomfortable around Joey and Tommy when I'm not around to hold her hand. She's not as direct and strong as Ramona.

"Don't worry Sam, I won't let these wolves have their way with her," Ramona said.

"I can take care of myself Ramona!" Connie fired back.

"Okay…I was just joking—sista'," Ramona said.

"I'll be right back, Connie. I don't think it's business related. As Miss Bernice and I head back to her office, I start to think what can be so urgent that Miss Bernice needs me all to herself. I paid the rent on time for next month. "Looks like you're gonna' have to make a decision about those two—and quick," she said. I stop in my tracks for a moment to laugh at what I just heard. "Your secretary has a crush on you fool," she reminded me.

"Connie? No damn way!" I said.

"Young man—Bernice knows affairs of the heart. That girl's in love with you. She let her hair down as a way of saying; Sam, here I am dammit! Come and get it." I laugh at Miss Bernice's "eloquent" way of describing the situation. "Is this what you wanted to see me about Miss Bernice?" I asked.

"No way Sam," she said. "I didn't want to bring this dirty laundry out in front of your friends."

Miss Bernice stops at the door to her office and turns around to face me. She shakes her head like the way a congregation would to a disgraced preacher. Now I'm worried. Miss Bernice looks me up and down and shakes her head again before turning around to open the door. As she opens the door I walk inside to see an Army Service rep stand up from Miss Bernice's couch with a handsome little Asian boy, looking at me with those big eyes of his. The kid looks up at the service man for something of a response. "What do we have here?" I asked, smiling. The little boy holds what looks like a photo in his tiny hand.

"Private First Class Phillips?" the service man asked, standing tall and saluting. I salute back—confused still. "That's me. But it's just Sam now soldier," I said. The soldier brings the little boy toward me close enough for him to hand me a picture he was clutching tightly. "This is your son, Sam," the soldier said softly. I stood there stoic and stunned beyond words. Miss Bernice was right. An announcement like this isn't something you just broadcast in front of everyone.

"You say what?"

"His name is Saivon. Saivon Phillips," the soldier said. I look at the picture the child handed me. It's a picture of me in my uniform with a beautiful Vietnamese girl I was seeing named Mai Nguyen. Mai and I met in a small restaurant in Saigon and instantly were attracted to one another. She and my buddies in my unit were the only things that kept me sane.

We always talked about her coming back to the states with me, but I couldn't find her after I got the call I was going home. They told me she had to move out of her last home because the North Vietnamese were coming in fast.

"What's your name soldier?" I asked.

"Corporal Reynolds, sir." I look Reynolds straight in the eyes—man to man for the right answer. "Is this for real, Reynolds?" Reynolds takes out a piece of paper from his briefcase and hands it to me. It's a Birth Certificate with my name on it as the boy's father. "What happened to Mai, Reynolds?" I asked, holding back tears.

"We don't know, sir. Last report is—during the fall of Saigon, it was a madhouse.

Helicopters were pulling on board as many people as possible. Reportedly she handed our guys Saivon's paperwork, and pictures of you two together. She said he was American. That was the last we heard of her. The North Vietnamese killed…well…a lot of people didn't make it Sam."

Chapter 25

A ton of emotions is filling me up like a punch in the gut from George Foreman. What am I going to do with a kid—I can't even take care of myself. I look down on the little boy to see if there's anything in him that I recognize. Does he have my eyes, my big nose—anything? "Saivon huh," I said. "The kid knows a little English, sir. His mother wanted him to be an American."

"How old are you, kid?" I asked, awkwardly. Saivon holds up four fingers to me, proudly. Corporal Reynolds smiles at Saivon, showing a bond that must that must have been needed—seeing he's lost his mother. "He's turning five in September, sir," Reynolds said. Saivon looks up and smiles at me. "Why wasn't I notified of this Corporal?"

"There were a lot of Amerasians born over there, sir. We notified as many as we could. Maybe the letter got lost in the mail." I look over at Miss Bernice who seems to be enjoying this "situation" I'm in. "So…what do I do now?" I asked. Corporal Reynolds hand me an army duffle bag I guess with the kid's clothing and personal items in it. "That's entirely up to you, sir. He's a good kid. They all are." Reynolds says his goodbye to Saivon and takes off—leaving me without so much as an instruction manual. I look at Miss Bernice, who laughs out loud this time. "Don't look at me soldier. You should have kept it in your pants." Now Miss Bernice takes off, leaving me with the kid—and the sound of crickets.

"Are you my daddy?" Saivon asked.

"I don't know kid, but we're sure going to find out." My father always told me; don't run from a hard fight—not a physical fight, but life because it builds character. "Always approach a good fight head on son," he would say.

"Are you hungry, Saivon?" I asked. He enthusiastically nods his head. "How about a fat American Cheeseburger?" Saivon jumps for joy in anticipation of his first American cheeseburger.

"Let's go kid." I take a deep breath and reach down for his hand. He slowly reaches up to grab my hand in a show of trust towards me as we head out the door.

In the bar, Ramona is getting restless, and ticked off that she's being put off by a man this long. She looks at her watch again for the third time in 5 minutes. "Left at the altar again, huh Ramona?" Joey asked, jokingly. Constance giggles while sipping her drink. "Shut up Joey!" she responds angrily. Miss Bernice walks in the room that peaks everyone's curiosity. "Miss Bernice, what the hell you have Sam doing—mopping the bathrooms to pay for his rent," Joey asked.

"No, yo' momma's back there with him—and she's a real pro'," Miss Bernice said. Miss Bernice's the queen of the "dozens". She doesn't care who you are—you crack a joke on her, and it's on baby. Everyone laughs except Ramona whose about to get up and leave when suddenly Sam and Saivon come out from the back. At this time, everyone's just a little inebriated and loose while slurring words. "Sammy.

Who's the cute kid?" Tommy asked. Not wanting to say anything in front of Saivon, I call Jack over to help out.

"Jack, get me a nice juicy cheeseburger for Saivon here," I said. "Put it on my tab." I hand Jack a two dollar tip that makes him frown. "Come on Sam, really?"

"What do you want from me? Do I look like Jay Rockefeller?" I hand him one more dollar for his trouble. "C'mon kid. Follow Uncle Jack."

Chapter 26

I guess it still hasn't sunk in yet that I might have a son as I watch Saivon walk with Jack, who takes Saivon back to the kitchen. I start walking over to the table like a good Catholic walking into Confession. "Sam—I could have been doing something else with my time tonight!" Ramona said in a huff. "Yes you could have Ramona, and I'm sorry for that. I'm going to have to call our evening short tonight. That cute kid that just went back to the kitchen maybe my son."

Needless to say, everyone is shocked—including Joey, who spits out his beer. "He's your son?!" Ramona asked. "Sam—you dog! You've been holding out on me?" Joey asked, stumbling over his words. I look over at Constance, who seems to be the only one who's not giving me their two cents. In fact—she smiles gracefully.

"That soldier who just left brought Saivon all the way from Saigon. He says I'm the father of that little boy," I said. Constance gently holds my hand to the disapproval of Ramona. "Where's the mother Sam?" she asked.

"They can't find her. She handed Saivon over to our forces doing the fall of Saigon." Joey finally tries to sober up a bit—being that he also was over there. "Damn bro'. I'm sorry to hear that," Joey said. "You think that I might have a little son or daughter coming too?"

"It's not contagious, Joey! I was in a real relationship with the boy's mother! I wanted to bring her home to the states, but I couldn't find her after we got the word that we were going home." Joey, always without the soft touch, gulps done another glass of beer, and added another five cents on the two cents he already gave. "You just should have hit it and quit—bro'. That's what we were told to do. Hit it and quit."

"Is that why there are thousands of Amerasian kids out there—bro!" I said, with slight angst.

"Take a blood test to be sure, Sam," Tommy said. "He could be some other soldier's son."

"Well…at least you know he's got a black daddy—with that nappy head of his," Ramona said with a dagger in her voice. If Ramona weren't a stone cold fox I wouldn't let her get away with such venom. You put up with a little bit more with a woman like her. Ramona finishes her drink and gets up from the table. "Well—it seems you're going to have your hands full Sam. You should have kept it in your pants." That's the second Black woman in less than 15 minutes to say I should have kept it in my pants. Some of these kids father's didn't make it back. I'll take this option to the alternative of coming home in a body bag. Ramona leaves, and I finish off my flat beer, not feeling like talking any more. "You guys can see your way out," I said. Tommy and Joey leave, holding on to each other as they stagger out of the bar. Constance stays behind, not saying a word as she watches me pick over cold fries.

Chapter 27

The Yokohama Black Rebels are having a good time
celebrating at a Japanese-owned nightclub with scantily clad
girls dancing with each other while middle-aged businessmen
eat sushi and other seafood off naked bodies. The music is
loud, and so are the Black Rebels. A secret meeting is being
held in the back offices with Hiroshi Ito sitting at the head of
the table. Hiroshi is the kind of man that speaks more with
his eyes than his mouth. A nod command will have several
people running to do his bidding—a cold stare can represent
the kiss of death.

Still a young man in his late twenties, Hiroshi is looking
to be the most powerful man in Japan. At the moment,
Hiroshi is none too pleased about what happened in the
afternoon. The young assassin who got killed at the police
station was rising in the ranks of the Black Rebels, which has
Hiroshi more upset than normal.

On the table are Saki, Sushi, rolls, and some other appetizers.

Some of Hiroshi's top Lieutenant's try to convince Him that they have the Yakuza running scared and that it will be a matter of time before they have Yamada's son. Hiroshi erupts—swiping his plate off the table in a single motion. "We don't have Yamada's son, do we?!" Hiroshi said in a rage in Japanese. "My best soldier is no longer here!" He was killed by someone of no importance! He was killed by a man who couldn't make it as a police officer!" The room goes silent as everyone listens to Hiroshi's tirade.

"The businesses are still reluctant to pay us protection money…!"

"We will get them all Boss Ito!" A suited man said, sitting next to Boss Ito.

"Really—and how will you do that?! You're not striking enough fear in their hearts! I want them to be afraid to wipe their asses without our consent!" A surprise guest is brought in by two of Hiroshi's men. The surprise guest is Johnny Tokoshima, Michelle Yamada's boyfriend. Johnny was "influenced" to come in and see Hiroshi.

Hiroshi's confidant whisper's in Hiroshi's ear that Johnny is here. Hiroshi's Saki is quickly replaced while he gets up to greet Johnny. He shakes Johnny's hand vigorously. "It's a pleasure to meet you, Boss Ito," Johnny said nervously.

"Johnny Tokoshima—you're the next Akira Kurosawa! I love your movies!" Hiroshi said like a prized groupie. Johnny looks around the room to see if there's a friendly face among the group. Not recognizing anyone he becomes even more suspicious of his "requested" visit. "I'm glad you enjoy my movies—but I don't understand why you requested me," Johnny said. Hiroshi's arm is draped around Johnny's neck like they were old high school buddies.

"Let's just say…I'm a big fan of yours—and your girlfriend."

"My girlfriend?" Johnny asked. Hiroshi nods his head in confidence like a man in his position should. "Yes…yes. I know your girlfriend just like I know your family." Hiroshi pulls out a picture of Johnny and Michelle and also a Polaroid of Johnny's family in Japan. Johnny is starting to get the understanding of what's going on. It's a shakedown he thinks.

He begins to worry—as he should. Hiroshi probably will not let Johnny leave without a mutual understanding.

"What do you want from me? I don't have much money," Johnny asked. Hiroshi laughs followed by his cronies and the girls to laugh as well.

"Don't worry about the money. If you say the wrong answer you won't be leaving here to tonight," Hiroshi insisted.

Chapter 28

Hiroshi takes Johnny over to his chair and sits him down at the head of the table. Hiroshi sits on top of the table with one leg hanging off. "Saki?" Hiroshi asked. Johnny shakes his head. Hiroshi takes the Saki himself and downs it in an instant. "I want to know the whereabouts of Michelle's little brother. You tell me this, and I'll let you and your family live." There aren't many options for Johnny other than going to the police, which will seal the fate of his family back home. "I don't know where her brother is—she doesn't mention him," he said. Hiroshi looks at one of his soldiers and gives him the nod. The young gangster walks over to Hiroshi and hands him a beautiful but deadly Katana Samurai sword. Several of Hiroshi's men grab Johnny and force him to his knees.

"Hold his arm out!" Hiroshi yells. The sadistic hoodlums comply—with laughter, as if it's a game. Johnny is sweating bullets and pleading for his life. "I don't know anything—I'm just a stupid movie director!"

"I don't care about your useless life or your family's back in Japan!" Hiroshi shouts. "Get me the information about the brother, and I want to know everything about the man who's protecting him!" Johnny begs for his life that amuses the sadistic Black Rebels. Hiroshi holds the weapon up in the air in a traditional striking pose.

"Okay…okay!" Johnny yells, looking at the shiny blade that could chop off his head in one quick slash. "Look—he pissed his pants!" One Rebel said, laughing. The men let Johnny up to gather what's left of his self-respect. Hiroshi holds the tip of the sword's blade against the Adams Apple of Johnny, prompting him to keep still. "You will report to me on a daily basis Johnny. Don't disappoint me." Johnny is led out of the room with his body intact, but his bladder in an uncontrollable mess.

The official letter finally arrived at my home that means that it definitely got lost. Saivon was a part of "Operation Baby Lift" an operation that went on in the final days of Vietnam. I take him to see my doctor for a full checkup. While the nurses are giving the kid all the candy he wants—he's already manipulating women, a chip off the old block. I talk to Dr. Mike Levine. "I have to commend you, Sam. I'm starting to see a lot of Amerasian children come through the doors, but mostly with Vietnam family members. You're one of the few American fathers that want anything to do with these kids. To most American soldiers they are an embarrassment for them—especially the ones that are married."

"Well...thankfully I'm not married Mike. I can see the embarrassment for a married couple, man—but hey, these kids are not at fault," I said. "Look at him in there—he's got those nurses eating right out of his hands." Dr. Mike continues to fill out paperwork as I look at Saivon in the next room. "How long will take for the results Mike?" I asked.

"Maybe a week—two at the most," Doc Mike said.

Chapter 29

As I drive back to the office with Saivon who is still smarting from more countless shots the poor kid must have gone through, my mind wanders a bit, thinking about his mother Mai. We had good times in a difficult war. Saivon seems to be a kid who sees the world half full. He seems to be unaffected by being away from his mother—for now.

Saivon points out the car at Mann's Chinese Theatre as tons of tourists take pictures of their favorite celebrities. I realize that now that I may have a son, my living arrangements may have to change. Saivon begins to play with my radio instruments. It's cute, but we have to lay down some ground rules. "Okay, son—never mess with a Black man's radio, son," I said. The kid just looks up at me and laughs.

We make it back to the office where Constance has a nice spread of lunch set up for us. She's surprised me with takeout from a Vietnamese restaurant of rice, noodles, vegetables, and pork. "What do we have here?" I asked as Saivon's eyes light up with anticipation.

"I wanted to do this for you after what happened the other day," Constance said. Keeping in the spirit of her new found makeover, Constance seems to be taking charge of her life—in a good way. I must admit it is a very attractive look on her. "Hi, Saivon!" she said with a big smile.
He smiles back but seems only interested in the food—I don't blame the kid. "Do you remember my name?" Constance asked.

"Connie!" Saivon said, boldly.

"That's right! Wow—you're a quick learner!" Connie fixes a small plate for him while I dig in myself. "You didn't have to go all out like this Connie," I said, while, of course, digging a hole in the noodles and pork bowls. "I wanted to do it—really," Connie said.

"I've seen on the news of the Amerasian kids that were left behind, being abandoned by the government there. It's sad." I take Saivon to his chair at a table that Connie put together. "Well…unfortunately he's not going to get any better treatment here in this country. He's Black and Asian, man—which of us will accept him?"

Connie looks back at Saivon, sitting and enjoying his food—using chopsticks that she gave him. She looks back at me with a look I've never seen before from her. "You will Sam!" she whispered forcefully. "He's your son…well…hopefully. What will you do if he's not your son—return him back to that terrible place?" I think about what Connie just said. She has a great point after all. Saivon's here because two people from different countries fell in love. But if he's not how can I just send the kid back to 'Nam. "Are you saying that I should adopt him?" I said. Connie opens a pair of chopsticks.

"People adopt all the time, Sam. That's just an option you have."

"Have you looked around Connie—The Jefferson's I'm not. I'm more like Sanford and Son, and that's what he'll be too." Connie giggles at the thought.

"That's funny."

"You're right that you can't stay here anymore," she said.

"There—you see?"

"So why don't you come and stay with me—for now," she said. As a man, what will you do when a beautiful young woman ask you and your son to move in with her. Run for the hills, or ask; how soon do you want us? "So we'll have our own little readymade family huh?" I asked.

"There're no strings attached," Connie said smiling. Now when that same beautiful, young woman comes out and says; there're no strings attached. There's usually strings attached. It's just a matter of how soon it'll begin, and how much it'll end up costing. "Let me think about it Connie."

"Don't think too long because I'm looking for a roommate soon."

Chapter 30

I left Saivon with Connie as I had to get back to doing my job. I'm sure Armstrong is anxious to take a break after pulling in a double for me. As I arrive at the "safe house" I notice a car parked in front of the house that I don't recognize. For one thing, it stands out like fish on a Sunday evening. A red Porsche in this neighborhood just doesn't happen much. I look around for suspicious behavior before heading up to the door with my hand on my gun. I turn the key and walk in slowly to see Michelle and a stranger having lunch with Ken and Armstrong.

"What's up Sammy?" Michelle asked. "Have some lunch?"

"No, thanks. Michelle—what's going on here?" The four of them are having KFC chicken and having a good time. Michelle has just broken a golden rule—bringing in an outsider to a safe house.

"I missed my little brother, so I thought I'd surprise him by stopping by and bringing lunch." Armstrong looks tired, but that doesn't stop him from slamming down a thigh and leg combination with biscuit.

"You brought in a stranger?" I said, trying not to show my anger. "You didn't get clearance from me. You've put us all in danger with this stunt!"

"This is Johnny—my boyfriend. He's an important movie director..."

"I don't care if he's the Emperor of Japan himself—I don't like surprises!" I yelled. "Armstrong, please come outside with me," I said. Armstrong gets up to follow me outside without saying a word. He looks as though he's a dead man walking to be the main attraction of an execution. "Armstrong—I'm going to give you a chance to explain yourself before I kick your ass all up and down this street, man!" I said, like an idiot

"C'mon Sam, you know you couldn't whup my ass— even on your best day," Armstrong said, looking down on me. "Well...well...in my mind I'm whupping your ass, man.

I'll be like a little Bulldog with my jaws attached to your Great Dane ass. I don't need to play a pissing game with you, Armstrong! You fucked up, big guy!" Armstrong lowers his head the way that I used to do when my father laid down the law with that stern voice. "I'm sorry Sam, Ken's sister was very convincing—"

"Yeah—she had a bucket of KFC, I can dig it man. You gotta' stop letting food control your life man," I said. "Look, she could have had those guys following her, and they would have shot up the neighborhood to get at that kid."

"I'm sorry boss. You were right, man. How can I make it up to you?" Armstrong asked.

"Go home and get some rest brother. You're going to need it. By the way, I have something for you." I open up a large brown case and open it up to display Armstrong's prized piece.

"That's my baby!" He shouts for joy. "You got my gun back!" Armstrong holds out the big Magnum to my horror. "Put the lion back in the cage…man!" I said, looking around. I send Armstrong on his way and head back in to clear up a few "misconceptions".

Chapter 31

Michelle tries to explain wanting to see her kid brother as her boyfriend seems distracted. I didn't think it would be a big problem to stop over to see my brother, Sam," Michelle said.

"It's not a big problem when you follow the rules Michelle," I answered back while going to the window and taking a peek out.

"She made a mistake, man!" Johnny blurts out, which catches Michelle off guard.

"Shut up Johnny! I can speak for myself!" Michelle hollered at him. I immediately go over to the table to take control of the situation before things get out of hand. "Listen my man—I don't know you, and I don't give a rat's ass.

Your girlfriend hired me to do a job, and me and my .45 here say I'm the best of us two to get the job done. If those bad guys bust in here are you going to stand up to them with harsh words or run for cover?" My point sinks in to Johnny as he sits back in his chair with his mouth shut.

"I'm glad you see it my way," I said. "Look Michelle— they've already tried once to kill Ken—almost tore up my car in the pursuit too. We can't afford to be taking things for granted."

"I understand Sam—it won't happen again," Michelle said.

"Good. Ken—what's up little buddy?" I asked. Ken gives me the Peace sign.

"I'm just hanging, Sam," he said with not a care in the world. Ken is a good kid. I can see why Armstrong has grown attached to him. It makes me wonder how he can be connected to a ruthless organization. Hell…even Al Capone had his good days.

The streets are red with blood in Little Tokyo, as the war between the gangs start to have an effect on local tourism in the area prompting the business owners to complain secretly to each other. But still they refuse to go to the authorities.

The Asian press is forcing the issue by reporting on the streets in front of businesses, causing alarm to the owners. "It's a gang war here in Little Tokyo that is striking fear in the business community and hurting tourism as well!"

A Japanese female reporter said. The business owner of an Import and Export store rushes out to stop the reporting. "Hey—what do you think you're doing?!" The man asked in a panic. "Do you want me to be next on their list?!" The reporter and the shop owner continue to argue over the issue as a crowd gathers around. Two young men walk up to the cameraman and knock the camera to the ground. One of the men walks up to the reporter and shows her his gun in his waistband. "The next time you are dead reporter," he said in Japanese. The man and his accomplice calmly walk away—blending into the crowd as the reporter tries to gather herself.

Chapter 32

Michelle and her boyfriend Johnny have left finally as Ken, and I have a couple of cold ones while we shoot the breeze. I checked in with Connie to make sure Saivon wasn't driving her crazy. I agreed to her proposal to move in with her, and by the sound of her voice I'd swear she was doing back flips.

I can't put my finger on it, but it was something about Johnny that raised my antennae. It was the way he kept looking away every time I looked at him. In my business, it pays to know how to read a person because what you know and don't know could get you in a lot of trouble. In a wolf pack, a submissive wolf would never look the alpha male in the eyes for fear of getting his ass kicked. Johnny's never met me so why would he be afraid?

"Ken, tell me what you know about your sister's boyfriend, Johnny?" I asked. Ken lets out a hard belch before he sets his beer down. "He's a total asshole!" Ken said with disgust. It looks as though Ken doesn't trust the guy as much as I do from the look on his face. "Tell me how you "really" feel kid," I said with sarcasm.

"I mean—he walks around like he's the next coming of Akira Kurasawa or something!"

"Akira who?" I asked. Ken gives me the same look that I gave him when I found out he'd never tried "Soul food".

"You've never heard of Akira Kurosawa?!" Ken asked with extreme shock.

"I guess I should be embarrassed by the look on your face," I said. Ken proceeded to tell me all about this director and some of the movies he's produced and directed. "He made the great movie "Seven Samurai" which was the inspiration for "The Magnificent Seven". That new movie "Star Wars" was another American movie inspired by a Kurasawa film," Ken said.

"I guess I'll have to get hip to his stuff," I said, wondering how the conversation changed to who's a better director. "How well do you know Johnny?" Ken hesitated for a moment—like he couldn't remember almost. "My sister never told me how long she's known Johnny. I just met him when I came back to America."

"So you don't know if he's Yakuza or Black Rebel?" I asked.

"He's definitely not Yakuza, and if he's Yokohama Black Rebel—he's had plenty of chances to kill me," Ken said. Ken finishes his beer and gives me a funny look. "Why are you asking questions about Johnny?" he asked. Seeing how Ken is getting suspicious I don't want to give him any reason to go to his sister about. If he tells Michelle, and Michelle confronts Johnny, all hell can break loose. "I'm just trying to be a good private dick, Ken. Everyone's a suspect in my book."

"I hate that I'm making all this trouble for everyone," Ken said. "You and Mr. Jones are sticking your necks out for someone you hardly know…" Ken chokes up and bows his head in Japanese tradition.

"Hey, I know your family, especially your mom. She was always there for my pop," I said. I pat Ken on the shoulder for support as I finish my beer. I get up to walk to the window to have a look see outside. The streets are alive out there—just the way I like it. There are not many surprises when the neighborhood is moving you dig. "Have you thought about what you want to do, now that you've left the gang?" I asked.

Something has touched off in Ken. He lights up when I asked him what he wanted to do with himself now. It was like it was the first time someone has asked him that—you know, like when an uncle or a family friend asks a child what they want to be when they grow up. I suppose his father the Yakuza boss never gave the poor kid an option.

"I love movies!" he said excited. "I always loved Toshiro Mifune movies—or Sonny Chiba! I think I'd make a good actor like them—doing action stuff!" Ken moves around doing martial art moves like I've seen on Kung Fu Theatre on Saturday mornings.

The kid's got some moves. "Oh, Sonny Chiba—I know him,"
I replied. "He's the cat they call "The Street Fighter! Yeah,
he's pretty cool. He's no Bruce Lee, but who in the hell is?"
And that's how we spent the rest of the afternoon. Talking
about cool kung fu movies and who are the baddest martial
art cats out there. It got pretty heavy when Ken said Sonny
Chiba would whup Bruce Lee's ass. What has he been
smoking?"

Chapter 33

Johnny makes his way to Little Tokyo to report to Hiroshi. He stops by Hiroshi's club and Sushi Bar, with exotic dancers dressed like schoolgirls, nurses, and any other fetish. Johnny arrives at the door where a very large Sumo Wrestler looking guy is standing. "I'm here to see Hiroshi," Johnny said. The large man remembers Johnny from the last meeting.

The bouncer pats down Hiroshi and then blows him a kiss. "He's in the back, sweet thing," he said. Johnny takes a long walk through the club—looking at all the excess eroticism and debauchery. Women flirt with him as he walks through the hall like a gauntlet.

In the hall leading to the back office, women are making out with each other and Black Rebel soldiers.

"Hiroshi?" Johnny asked. A man points to the back without looking up from taking care of his "business". Johnny makes it to the office as scantily clad girls come out fixing their clothes. Johnny meekly walks in and quickly turns his head at what he sees. Hiroshi is banging two girls out in the open surrounded by other girls and his bodyguards. "What's up Johnny, my man?!" Hiroshi shouts, out of breath. "Come in…my friend. Hiroshi gets up from his conquest like he was a king of a large harem.

He wipes off with a white towel given to him by a bodyguard named Hadeo. Hadeo is Hiroshi's closest confidant who walks with a limp from an attempted assassination of Hiroshi. "I take it you have news for me, Johnny," Hiroshi said.

"I have the Private Detective's location where he's hiding Ken Yamada," Johnny said. Hiroshi pat's Johnny on the shoulder as he walks him over to his big desk. Hiroshi pulls out a big bottle of whiskey and pours a glass. He gives the glass to Johnny and drinks from the bottle himself. Johnny slowly picks up the glass—looking straight through the bottom as if he sees his self respect in there.

He finally gulps it down real fast.

"Wow, you must have had a lot of worries on your mind Johnny!" Hiroshi said mockingly. Hiroshi pours Johnny another glass. "So, how is the movie business doing?" Hiroshi asked. Johnny, aggravated, quickly downs the drink. "I thought you wanted the location!" Hadeo, hearing the tone in Johnny's voice pulls out a switchblade and limps over to Johnny. He pins him down and is ready to cut off Johnny's left ear. Hiroshi waves Hadeo off just in time. "I can appreciate your frustration Johnny. A man in your position is not used to taking orders from someone. You give them. You must have a very low opinion of me. Hadeo lets Johnny up off the desk. Hiroshi fixes Johnny's shirt and collar. "I own you now Johnny. As long as you—as the Americans say, play ball, your family will not be harmed."

"I'm sorry Hiroshi. Please forgive me," Johnny pleads. Another young Japanese girl cozy's up to Hiroshi. "You will give Hadeo here the location of that meddling Private Detective, and then you will sit down and tell me more about the movie industry."

Chapter 34

Mayor Paul Jefferson holds a press conference on the steps of the courthouse with police chief Robert Ironside and Captain Pierpont at his side. With the recent murders in Little Tokyo affecting tourism, the mayor is taking the heat—and in an election year that spells trouble for an incumbent. The press you might say is in full riot gear and is ready to take some shots at the three officials. Reporters from various news outlets push and shove, all to get the mayor's attention.

"Mayor—what are you doing to stop the violence in Little Tokyo?!" one reporter shouts out.

"Mayor—you once said the buck stops with you—should you now step aside?!" another asked. Reporters are firing questions at the mayor in rapid fire succession. Mayor Jefferson waves his hands to try and get some order from the rabid crowd.

"We are doing everything humanly possible to stop this outrageous violence in Little Tokyo that's hurting the business community there. I've communicated with Police Chief Ironside and Captain Pierpont to organize a task force designed to bring down these crime organizations. The police brought Al Capone and the Chicago Mob to justice, we can do the same there."

"It was the IRS that brought Capone to justice," a cigar chomping veteran reporter said. Mayor Jefferson, slightly embarrassed, jumps back to answer his critic. "It was a joint effort sir! The IRS along with the strong police leadership of agents like Elliot Ness!" he said strongly.

Nancy Sayama, a Japanese reporter representing the community is jockeying for position on the front row. Nancy has the look of a high fashion runway model—but don't you be fooled. She's had tussles with the Yakuza and has lived to tell about it. Some in the community call her the Little Dragon Lady because of her fierce conviction. "Stop pushing lady!" A jerk reporter said to Nancy. "Shouldn't you be at home cooking sushi for your husband?" he asked arrogantly.

"First of all—you don't cook sushi asshole! Second—
your breath need some much-needed relief." Nancy moves
past the little man like a stiff-armed defensive back on her
way to a touchdown. "Mayor Jefferson—when will both
Chinatown and Little Tokyo have more Asian policemen
patrolling the streets?!" she asked. The mayor quickly
confers with Police Chief Ironside before getting back on the
microphone. "The Police Chief has assured me that the task
force being assembled will have young Asian recruits ready
to patrol their communities," he said. Ironside steps up to the
microphone to assist Mayor Jefferson. "These are young and
well-trained recruits who are not influenced by the old
traditions of the communities," Ironside said. "Think of them
as the newer version of the "Untouchables" you might say."

"And when does this go into effect, Mayor?" Nancy
asked, seemingly satisfied with the good news. "Next week
the recruits go out with their experienced partners, ma'am,"
Captain Pierpont intercedes. Happy with the outcome, Nancy
gives the thumbs up sign to her cameraman.

Chapter 35

I followed my gut feeling that something was going to happen tonight, so to be cautious, I sent Ken to Manny's place in the city of Hawthorn. I called upon Armstrong to back me up, and he practically arrived before I could hang up the phone. Armstrong is like a caged lion that yearns to go on a big hunt. He's itching for a fight. If he lived back in Ancient Rome, he'd be a prized gladiator.

While I watch the front door, Armstrong is sitting on the floor across from me and watching the back door. Sitting in the dark, we make the best of the quiet time. "You sent poor Ken to Manny's huh Boss?" Armstrong asked jokingly. "Manny will probably try to adopt Ken and put him to work right away." We both laugh because we know how Manny is. He's worked very hard to get where he is, and he expects people to have the same work ethic.

The sound of crickets is the only things that can be heard on a sweltering night until I hear the sound of paper being unwrapped. "Armstrong—what the hell are you doing man?!" I asked with a strong whisper. "I missed lunch today brother. Do you want some?"

"I'm glad you didn't go to 'Nam man. That little act could give the whole unit's position away. I need you to be sharp big guy." Armstrong takes a guilty "bite" of a chip that could bust an eardrum. He gets the hint that the sound of a Lays chip just too noisy. He closes the bag that causes even more noise. "Is there any news about your son?" Armstrong asked, trying to change the subject. "I'm supposed to hear something tomorrow."

"Which direction do you want the results to go?" Armstrong asked, leaning up against the wall as he checks his gun for the umpteenth time. "Will you stop checking your gun fool?! You're making me nervous dammit!"

"I'm sorry Sam—I can't stand the waiting. I guess I wouldn't have made a good soldier," Armstrong said. "Fuck it, man—you wouldn't have been any worse than any of us man. There were no John Wayne's out there brother. We were the super power, but they kicked our ass using tactics we didn't anticipate. So now I take little colored pills to cope. But I just keep on truckin' man."

"I can dig it, Sam. Hey, maybe your kid can follow in your footsteps the way you followed your father's footsteps to be a Private Investigator."

"I guess we'll just have to wait and see," I said. Suddenly, a noise coming from the front door area got my attention. I hold up my hand to Armstrong to get his attention. We get up from the floor and ready ourselves for what's outsides those doors.

The doorknob slowly turns but is locked. After what seemed like an eternity, a burglary tool is used to open the door. The door opens letting in the moonlight from a full moon. Three men creep in wearing black to blend in with the night as I see from their silhouettes that they were carrying some big guns. I wait for the last man to get inside before I give Armstrong the signal on three.

"Throw your weapons down assholes!" I shouted.

All hell breaks loose as the safe house becomes 'shootout at the OK Corral'. The walls are littered with bullet holes as Armstrong sticks his cannon out and blasts one of the hoodlums up against the wall. A semi-automatic Mac 10 is sprayed our way that takes out a window. We return fire as I unload my clip into the last two gangsters. One of the men falls dead as the other limps—running out the door. "I got'em Sam!" Armstrong yelled, chasing after the injured man. "ARMSTRONG! Dammit!" I shouted loudly. It doesn't look good for a Black Man as big as Armstrong to running down the street at night with his big cannon.

Crazy Armstrong fires another shot at the assassin as he dives into a waiting vehicle. If the gunfire inside the house didn't wake up the neighborhood that last shot sure as hell did.

Part Three

Revenge is Best Served Cold

Chapter 36

Captain Pierpont and the gang are all present at the scene, going over my safe house with a fine tooth comb. Pierpont has come out of the office to take a personal interest because of the politics involved. Crime scene tape is put around the doors as the neighborhood comes alive in the darkness. Patrol cars are lined up blocking off any traffic trying to get through. Pierpont, who enjoys using me as his penyata, is chomping on his cigar while giving me the big stare down while Armstrong is being questioned by officers.

Joey and Tommy are looking over the bodies while the Crime Scene cats do their thing.

"Give me the story Phillips, and it better be a good one!" Pierpont snapped. "We've got two dead men shot full of holes—in your place!"

"Hey, we got one alive over here!" Joey shouts. Pierpont and I race over to the kid whose spitting up blood. Pierpont bends down with his arthritic left knee—grimacing as gets in the kid's painted face. "Who sent you kid?" he asked. The kid starts to smile even while coughing and gagging for air as he speaks in Japanese. "Tommy—what's he saying dammit?" Pierpont asked. "He's saying that the Yokohama Black Rebels are here to stay and that Sam is a dead man. His days are numbered." The young gangster points at me with his fingers mimicking a gun and pulls the trigger. He dies without giving out information.

Pierpont looks up at me with disgust—why I don't know. "Okay, that's it, Phillips! You're going in before the people around you start dropping dead! And that means bringing in that kid they're after! Why is he so important to them?

"It's a civil war Captain," I said. "It's their own North against the South with a little bit of revenge thrown in." Tommy stands up with a pained look on his face after watching the kid die. He loosens up his tie like a businessman after a long day at a 9 to 5. "He couldn't have been any more than eighteen years old," Tommy said.

132

"Look around partner. These assholes made this place look like the Alamo. He's no angel ova' here," Joey said. Joey's comment seemed to get a rise out of Tommy, whose maybe had enough of Joey's sometimes racist comments towards Asians. "The Yakuza were in power for a long time partner—even longer than the Mafia. They were bound to piss off the wrong people someday. The Black Rebels stood up against them when no one else would."

"It seems like you admire them to me Tommy," Joey said in a direct tone. "Who side are you on?"

"I admired the Native Americans for rising up against the onslaught of White settlers taking over their land—and we all know what happened there don't we? Yes, I admire the Black Rebels, but eventually they'll be defeated. History is not on their side."

"Thanks for the history lesson, partner but I just need to know you'll have my back when the shit goes down," Joey said. Joey stares down Tommy waiting for an answer.

"What the fuck you think Joey? I'm a cop man!"

"Fuckin' A you are!" Joey snapped. While Joey and Tommy have their lover's quarrel, Pierpont hasn't forgotten about me. "I'm still waiting for the story Phillips," he said.

I take a moment to gather my thoughts because this bulldog wants to clamp down on my ass if I say anything that doesn't jive with him. "I had a hunch Captain, so I moved on it. I got my client out of harm's way, and when we came back to get some more things we needed we got attacked by theses assassins. It was self-defense." The captain, of course, wasn't buying it of course, but hey what's he going to do—arrest the men that killed some known killers.

"You had a hunch huh Phillips?" Pierpont asked suspiciously. "I ought to run you and your boy here for coming up with such a bullshit story! Bring your client in and let the police handle it! Do we understand each other Phillips?!"

"Now Captain—I was paid to do a job. You knew my dad. Would he ever turn his back on a client? I don't think so."

"Lou—throw the cuffs on Phillips and the big fella' over there!" Pierpont snapped.

"You're cuffing me on what charges?!" I asked emphatically.

"On obstruction!" Pierpont replied. "You think about what you're doing while you spend some time in the "can" smart ass!"

Chapter 37

For his total dislike of me, Captain Pierpont had me thrown under the jail with some of the roughest characters in Los Angeles. The captain also thought he was adding insult by not charging Armstrong so he couldn't be my back up. He wants to send a message to me who was in charge. The desk sergeant, an ass-hole by the name of O'Halloran comes in finally after I've been asking for my phone call for an hour now.

"Okay Phillips, you can make that call now," he said with a big smug look on his round face. O'Halloran's been on the job for thirty years. Back when the Los Angeles Police were at their worst when it came to racial integration and harmony. It was a shoot first philosophy among the brothers in blue, and O'Halloran was neck deep in it. He gave my father a hard time of it, so I guess he's keeping the tradition going.

"Why thank you Sergeant," I said as he opens the cell. "By the way O'Halloran—would you give me a drink of water on my death bed?"

"If I was at your death bed it would be to pull the plug, Phillips."

"No more Christmas cards for you, sir," I said with sarcasm. O'Halloran rolls his eyes as he heads off to darken someone else's day. I place a call to Constance, who must be wondering where in the hell I am, and I must admit I do miss Saivon. "Hello," Constance said.

"Connie—it's Sam."

"Hi boss. Where are you?" Constance asked, with concern in her voice.

"I'm in jail. I'll explain later. Take a look outside— Armstrong should be parked out there." Constance peeks through her curtains. "Yes I see him. What's going on?" Constance asked.

"Let's just say that the bad guys tried to get a two for one tonight but failed. How's Saivon?" I asked. "He's a great kid, Sam. I had read him a story before he crashed on the sofa." I can hear the smiling tone in Constance's voice that lets me know that Saivon's in good hands.

"I don't know what I would do without you Connie," I said.

"You just remember that when it's time for me to get a raise," she added. O'Halloran is making his way back down—I'm sure to kick me off the phone, so I'd better wrap things up with Constance. Connie, this gang that's looking for Ken will do everything they can to get their hands on him. Take a few days off until this all blows over," I said.

"Be careful, and...don't drop the soap," she jokes. All I can do is laugh as I forgot how weird Constance's humor could be. "Alright Phillips—times up, O'Halloran said. "I'm sure your cellmates miss you," he added, laughing obnoxiously. O'Halloran pushes me back inside and slams the bars shut while laughing at me with that shit face of his.

"Hey, when am I'm gonna' get out of here, O'Halloran?

"When the captain says so, fresh meat!" he snickered. The sergeant returns to his nest upstairs to leave me with a cage full of undesirables looking to make a name for themselves before they get transferred to the joint. And I'm at the top of their list. One extremely large dude who is so dark when they say black and blue, his picture would pull up.

I'm sure he's not looking for a rep' because he probably has them all. "Hey, brother, that's a fine suit you have on," he said, standing over me so large I couldn't see around him. "Thanks," I replied, carefully while trying to take a seat. "I want it—Jive Turkey," he ordered without raising his voice. A man like him don't need to. I step to one side to look around him for help from the other guys who seem to all be missing at least one garment or two. They look away quickly

"It's like that?" I ask them. I begin to start taking off my suit jacket, and suddenly I get a rush of bravery in me. I drop the coat on the floor, and while the goliath is distracted looking down, I slug him in the face, but all I hurt was my hand. "Shit!" I said out loud.

"That tickled," he said with a smile showing one gold tooth. He grabbed me and tossed me across the cell like a rag doll. I knew I was in for a long night, so I might as well give this big mutha' fucka' a show he won't forget.

Chapter 38

The next morning I was released—a little battered and bruised, but my dignity intact. I even got to keep my suit on even though it's ripped to shreds. The captain had a heart after all in releasing me, but I think it goes a little deeper than that. My guess is he knows as long as I'm on the street and protecting Ken, the Yokohama Black Rebels will come out of hiding and will eventually make a mistake. That also can happen on my end too. I can't go on protecting the kid forever. Something's got to break soon.

I make a quick stop to Dr. Levine's office to get the results I've been waiting on which has me more nervous than facing that big "John Henry" looking dude from last night. I sit in the office and wait my turn while getting stared at by a weirdo professor looking man and a woman who's reading the book "Shogun" By James Clavell. "I bet I know what you here for," the weirdo said.

"I'm sorry, are you talking to me?" I asked, knowing all the time that he is. "You're here for a sexually transmitted disease aren't you?" he asked like a raving pervert. Maybe it's because of my ragged and unshaven look. "Uh, no I'm not my man—I'm on an undercover case, so let's keep this between me and you," I said.

"What about her?" he asked pointing over at the woman reading quietly, as she looks up from her book. "Who you're working for—CIA, DEA, FBI?" he asked in rapid succession. Whoa—look at the time I said to myself, looking at my watch. I don't have a book like the young lady does, so I start looking for something to read from the magazine collection. "Mr. Phillips, the doctor will see you now," the medical assistant said. I follow her to Dr. Levine's office where he's looking at me with a big smile on his face.

"Sam, how's it going?" he asked as we shake hands.

"I'm wandering about that weird guy you have out in the lobby, Doc."

"That's Douglass Preston. He's a reclusive millionaire who also happens to be a hypochondriac," the doctor explains. The lady out there is his assistant."

It all makes sense now to me. It seems to be the richer you are, the more it makes you move to the edge of insanity. The same thing happened to Howard Hughes. They didn't even go to war—well, most of them. What demons did they have to fight? You have those results for me Mike?" The good doctor hands me the file. I look at all the data showing Saivon and my blood work. "Does this mean what I think it is Mike?" I asked.

"I sure do. You're a 99.9% match with Saivon," Dr. Levine said. "Congratulations."

The results confirmed what I already knew in my heart. I'm a father. I walk out of the doctor's office to the lobby and stop at the lady reading her book. "That seems like an interesting read," I said.

"It is," she said.

"I'll give you ten dollars for it." The woman contemplates hard for about a minute.

"Okay," she agreed, handing over the book. Shogun is a bestselling book on Japan's culture. I figure I can learn about my enemy's background.

Chapter 39

I open the door to Connie's apartment with an extra key she gave me. Connie greets me like a husband and father coming home from a hard day's work. "Hi Boss," Constance said with a smile on her face. She grabs my hat and places it on a coat rack. "Hello, Mr. Sam? Miss Connie fixed me breakfast! I left some for you also."

"You did huh?" I asked. I stooped down to Saivon's level so I could look him in the eyes. "Call me Daddy," I said. It finally sank into me. I know I should have trusted Mai from the time Saivon walked in, but a man's pride is his strength and his weakness. "Okay Daddy." I look around Constance's place for the first time doing the daytime and realize that it's a cool looking crib. "I guess the results were what you wanted after all?" Constance asked.

"Yes they were Connie. I'm going to need a lot of help raising him," I said. Connie's eyes perk up at the idea. "I could help out any time!" she said with enthusiasm.

"That's okay Connie. It's time the kid met his new grandmother. Besides, I can't impose on you forever." "It's no problem Sam. I like little Saivon."

"Connie, you're a beautiful sista', and you've been a great help in the office…but this domestic thing with us can't work—you know that right?" I asked. "A man in my field don't do well being tied down. Also—I live out of my office baby, what do I have to offer anyone?" Connie gives me a big smile, but I can tell she's disappointed. "Boss—it's in my nature to help out. That's the way I was brought up. I've seen the women that have come in and out of your life, including that Ramona woman. I'm not in their league."

"Good—I'm glad we've got that settled."

"Me too," Connie said. We stand in silence for a moment; both of us not knowing what to say next. "I'll have the phone company transfer the calls here, so you don't need to go in for a couple days," I said.

"I've already done that, Boss. No messages so far. Saivon is watching cartoons—oblivious to the grownup's conversation.

144

He laughs out loud while watching Bugs Bunny and Elmer Fudd. We both smile at Saivon, who seems to be adjusting just fine. "He's a smart boy, Boss. Have you thought about schooling yet?" she asked. After Connie had said those last words, I feel as though I was just kicked in the gut by a mule. I haven't given school a thought at all. What kind of father am I going to be if I don't think about his education?

"I'm sorry. I haven't had a chance to think about that yet with the case heating up," I said. Connie goes to the living room and brings back a folder. "I made a few phone calls to area schools just in case. You have to contact them early at Saivon's age." She hands over the folder to me while I stand here feeling like an idiot.

Chapter 40

I showered and shaved to get the stench of a night spent in jail had on me as I take the kid to go see his grandmother for the first time. I haven't had a chance to tell my mother about Saivon yet—maybe I was too afraid, but it's not something you just blurt over the phone. I thanked Armstrong for watching Connie's apartment by giving him a box of Donuts, including his favorite—chocolate and vanilla Long Johns. I asked him to meet over at Manny's place after he knocks off for a couple hours. Sleep. That sounds like a foreign word to me right now, as I have yet to have a decent night of it since I've taken this case.

I look over my shoulder at Saivon to make sure he's okay, and he gives me a big smile as if to tell me everything's cool Dad. Connie did a great job on Saivon's hair which is jet black, thick and curly.

"We're going to see your Grandmother Son. Do you like that?" I asked.

"Yes," he said.

"You say, yes sir, okay. Always say, yes sir, yes ma'am, especially when talking to Grandma."

"Yes sir," Saivon said.

"That's my boy." We finally arrive in Long Beach and my mother's place just after the lunch rush—a perfect time to sit down with my mother. Butterflies are forming in my stomach as I get out the car. I go around and help Saivon out of his seat as my mother is saying goodbye to her last lunch guest before she closes. She sees me and waves, and then has a funny look on her face as Saivon comes from around the car, catching her attention. I straighten his clothes and then grab his hand as I take baby steps toward the restaurant like a scared sinner walking down the aisle of a Pentecostal church. At times, my mother is like a fiery preacher laying her hand on your head.

"Hi Momma," I said sheepishly. My mother was in the choir of a Pentecostal church, so I anticipate her giving me the "word" about what's led me having a grandson come into her life that she didn't know about. "What's up son? Is this Ken's little brother?" she asked.

147

I can tell she doesn't believe this is Ken's little brother, but it's just her way that's all. "This is Saivon, Momma," I answered back. "Can we come in? I need to talk to you."

"You don't need to ask me to come in son. You're family." I hope she means that after what I have to tell her. We go inside, and while he is enjoying a bowl of peach cobbler and ice cream, I sit down with my mother and break the news about Saivon. Needless to say, she's not taking it too well. "He's your son?! He looks Asian," she snapped

"Look closely Momma. He has my nose, smile and kinky hair. His mother was a woman I saw for most of my tour there, and she got him out of Saigon when it fell. I also had us blood tested." My mother looks at Saivon sitting across the room sitting with a waitress who's keeping him entertained. "You don't even have a woman in your life to help raise him. And on what you're earning how can you support him?!"

"I'm taking on more cases now and I might take on work at law firms now that I have a son to raise," I said, trying to convince her or am I trying to convince myself. My father hated working for law firms. They treated him like a butler he said.

Times are changing though, and cases are getting bigger and bigger that needs investigative know how. Hell, maybe this can work out. "I'm going to find him a good school. Connie wants to help out as well."

"Now there's a good young Christian girl. You ought to be knockin' on her door."

"I dig where you're coming from Momma. When I'm ready to jump the broom, she'll be on the list," I joked. "He's your Grandson, Momma. I was hoping he could spend time with you also—at least until I can find a babysitter," I said. Another waitress joins in with Saivon.

"Well…he's sure making an impression on the girls," Momma said.

Chapter 41

I dropped Saivon off at Connie's place as I meet up with Armstrong at Manny's place in Sun Valley, just north of North Hollywood. Sun Valley is the hottest place in the San Fernando Valley, but when it rains there, the water can reach above your knees. Manny has a nice home there—one of two that he owns.

His wife Rosie makes good money Manny told me working as an in-home nurse. They have two sons—Miguel and Julio, and a young daughter named Carmen. Ken seems to be quite comfortable with his living arrangements as he enjoys some homemade Enchiladas which of course Armstrong has to have some.

"Manny—you holding out on us, my man?" he asked.

"Armstrong—amigo, I've invited you over many times for some Authentic Mexican food," Manny said.

"Well…here I am amigo!" While Armstrong helps himself and jokes with Ken, I talk things over with Manny.

"What do I owe you Manny?" I asked. Manny pushes my wallet away quickly. "Your money's no good here Sam," he said. "Your father was always kind to me, and he always made sure he sent customers over to me when I first started out. And he was very proud of you.

"Thanks, Manny." As we watch Armstrong and Ken munch on Enchiladas like as if joined at the hip, I couldn't help but be envious of what Manny has accomplished. "Was there any drama from the kid?" I asked.

"Oh no, he's no problem. I've seen kids like him all the time—in gangs, and trouble at home. They just need someone in their life that can show them a positive influence that's all. He's a good kid."

"This case has to end soon Manny. I can't put friends like you in harm's way. These guys will do anything to get Ken.

Maybe I'm going about this the wrong way." I've been playing defense all this time. Maybe it's my time to go on the attack—shake things up a bit. First I need to give Michelle some news that she's not going to like. "Ken, Armstrong— we need to book, I said in a hurry. Armstrong and Ken wipe their mouths of sauce as I finally have the answer I was looking for. "Manny—thanks for everything. I'll be in touch.""Any time Sam." As we walk outside to our cars, Armstrong is just as curious as Ken on what's going on in my head. "What's up Boss?" Armstrong asked.

"Take Ken to your place A.J. Those guys wouldn't dare step foot in Compton," I said.

"And where are you headed?" Armstrong asked.

"I have that meeting with you know who." Armstrong knew exactly who I was referring to. The sooner she knows, the quicker this ordeal can end.

Chapter 42

I made a phone call to Michelle for her to meet me for coffee and discuss the case. I got word from Joey that the task force has found the Black Rebel Crime boss' place, and are moving to take out the gang tomorrow. He asked me if I wanted to tag along as an observer since it's my client that they want to take out. How Joey got Captain Pierpont's approval, I don't know, but it's a chance for me to look this bastard who wants to kill me, straight in the face. Michelle finally arrives alone just as I requested. A smile comes across her face as her eyes meet mine. A lifetime ago we probably could have set the world on fire, but I was a kid who wanted to make something of his self, and I thought the army could do that for me. The jury is still out on that. "How are you Sam?"

"Michelle—good to see you," I said, greeting her with a hug.

The coffee shop is a nice little café in Studio City, which has outdoor seating.

The waitress comes outside with her pencil and menu. They say if you wait long enough while sitting down in Studio City, a famous person will walk by soon. "Coffee—black, sweetheart," I said.

"I'll have coffee with cream and sugar and a croissant please," Michelle said.

"I'll be right back," the waitress said. The waitress heads to another table before going back inside. "I wanted to give you an update on what's happening in the case," I said. Michelle gets out her checkbook also as it's time for a payment for my services. "How are things going?" she asked. "There was another attempt on Ken's life the other night Michelle. Three Black Rebel assassins came to my safe house with automatic weapons and shot the place up.

"Oh my God—is he alright?!" Michelle asked with concern.

"He's okay. Doing this work gives you certain instincts. I had concerns when you came to visit the safe house last week with your boyfriend."

"Johnny? What does he have to do with this?" Michelle asked. The coffee arrives to interrupt the conversation for a moment. We wait for the waitress to finish her business before continuing. "Can I get you folks anything else?" she asked politely. I break off a five dollar bill from my money clip and hand it to the waitress. "Keep the change sweetheart."

"Thank you!" The waitress goes off to her other table giving us the privacy we wanted.

"No one else knew about the safe house except you, Ken, and now Johnny. I think he is either connected to this gang or was compromised somehow, baby."

"Maybe you were followed Sam. Your car sticks out big time!" Michelle said, a little angry. "I could be wrong sweetheart, but I doubt it. You hired me to protect your brother, and I'm the best in the business. If I didn't do what I did, Ken would be in a morgue downtown, and so would I."

I give her a moment to let it sink in that her boyfriend is not to be trusted. Other than a man sleeping around on you, this sort of betrayal is hard to take.

"I'll kill him myself!" Michelle snaps while stirring sugar in her coffee.

"No—don't do that," I said. "Besides, I'm sure he was threatened. That's how these gangs operate. You just stay away from him for a while until this blows over."

"And then what?" Michelle asked.

"Then you can have at him—after I'm through whupping his ass."

Chapter 43

Later that night back at Connie's place, I was so tired I was out like a light as soon as my head touched the pillow on Connie's pull out sofa. Saivon is sleeping in the other bedroom. Unfortunately, that didn't stop my nightmares from staying away. Tossing and turning, my demons from the war have come back.

Bombs are going off in my head, causing my head to ache as if it's being run over by a locomotive. "NO!" I shout, waking up in a cold sweat. Connie rushes out to see me soaking wet. I've never told her about my nightmares because it may cause her to look at me with pity. "Sam, are you okay?!" Connie asked. She down next to me on the sofa bed wearing a black nightgown, and smelling with a fragrance I've never smelled before.

"I'm fine—it's nothing," I said, trying to convince her. She feels my forehead that is now dripping all over her sheets. "You're burning up, Boss. Let me get you some water," she said, rushing into the kitchen. Walking away from me, Connie looks totally different I must say, especially without her glasses and no war paint on. I quickly look around for my pills that are in my pants that seem to have walked across the room. The pants might as well be on the other side of the world—undiscovered territory you might say as I don't want my secretary to find me standing there butt naked.

Connie returns with the water in the dim lit room. The shiny night gown, glistening in the light has sobered me up more than those damn pills could ever do. "Drink this," she said. "I added a slice of lemon to it." I gulp it down, which I admit hit the spot, which is now what I want to do to Connie—hit her spot. "Where you having a nightmare Sam?" she asked, touching me on the forehead, and then moving her hand around my face and neck. "I'm okay Connie—the water hit the…I mean the water was what I needed."

"Sam—I know you were in the Army in Vietnam. I read all the stories of battle fatigue, Agent Orange, and other horrible stuff."

"Oh, you do huh?"

"Sure. I had a cousin and an Uncle over there. They're heavy drug users now," Connie said. Her hand keeps going south on my chest, down my tank top t-shirt

"Connie, we can't…"

"Shut up. I want to," Connie said forcibly. Connie slides my t-shirt over my head, as she kisses my chest. And I did hit her spot—for the rest of the night.

Chapter 44

It's show time, as the summer nears its end on a sunny Friday morning. The task force has located Hiroshi Ito and his gang in a mansion in Alhambra—a county of Los Angeles. A Little Tokyo merchant has finally come through to tell of prostitution, drugs, and murder going on and has had enough. In conjunction with the Alhambra police force, the task force consists of new Asian plain clothes officers along with the Asian Gang Unit of Joey, Tommy, Maria Ozawa, Charles Thompson, and Fred "Downtown" Washington.

Stationed a block away in hidden vehicles, we wait for the word to come through. I get a smile from Joey who seems to be enjoying this moment, as he and Tommy give each other "five".

"Let's rock and roll Tommy!" Joey said with gusto. Tommy adjusts his bullet-proof vest as he fires himself up—taking a deep breath. "It's just like old times, hey Sam?!" Joey asked.

I nod my head as I watch everyone go through their rituals. "Yeah…old times, man." Maria, Charles, and Fred are in another van while the other gang units occupy others.

"Sam, don't try to engage with these bastards. We got it covered, okay?" Joey said.

"Oh, don't worry about that. I'm in no hurry to be a hero my friend." Both vans keep in touch with radios as the big house is being monitored. "Charlie—you see anything on your end?" Joey asked while Tommy looks through his binoculars.

"Negative. We're flying blind here, man. No one has a photo of this guy. He's ghost brother."

"Sit tight gentlemen. We're waiting for the big guy to show up," a voice cuts in on the radio that I don't recognize. "Who's that?" I asked.

"That, my friend is the Task Unit boss—Detective Jack Hawkins. His friends I heard call him Nails. He makes Captain Pierpont look like Barney Fife," Tommy said. I chuckle at the thought of that, so does Joey. "So Sammy, how's that new kid of yours doing?" Joey asked with a sly smile. I know that look from Joey—acting like his shit doesn't stink. He's banged dozens of Vietnamese whores over there. I'd be willing to bet that he caught a sexually transmitted disease or two. "He's doing fine Joey," I said. "He's officially my son. He's a good kid."

"Oh, I'm sure the kid's never had it so good man," Joey said.

"What's that supposed to mean, Brotha'?

"I'm just sayin' you know…coming from 'Nam and all."

"Joey, I'm starting to realize why you got your ass kicked so many times as a kid." Tommy starts to laugh which makes Joey angry. "Okay paison. Your ex, Ramona and me are knocking boots now," he said with a callous bravado. We push and shove each other around causing Tommy to separate us. Hell, I really didn't give a damn about him and Ramona.

It's Joey's pompous Italian Stallion thing that gets under my skin. My feelings for Ramona changed the minute Saivon came into the picture, and she was less than cordial towards the kid.

Chapter 45

Cooler heads prevail as I realize why I was here in the first place. Besides, Joey is Joey, man. He was the same guy I met in country. You have to take the good with the bad with Joey. "Looks like we're on boys and girls," said Detective Hawkins, as a Black Mercedes rolls up with tinted windows surrounded by two other cars. "Shit—tinted windows!" Hawkins shouts. "Everybody stay cool." All the units watch as the motorcade makes its way through the gauntlet without knowing what's happening. The vehicles make their way into the driveway one at a time as Hawkins and his team, try to recognize Hiroshi.

Hawkins's man, Rico Santiago, looks at the photo of Hiroshi given to them by the informant. All the Japanese men are dressed to the nine's in dark suits like they're pallbearers at a funeral. "Which one is he?!" asked Detective Hawkins, perspiring in the crowded van.

Everyone is looking for a signal from Detective Hawkins who can't make a positive I.D. "What the fuck is this guy waiting on?!" asked a frustrated Joey.

"Rico—is it him or not?!"

"I...I'm not sure Jack," Rico said. The gangsters make it inside to the frustration of the units—angry at Hawkins for not pulling the trigger on the raid. "Fuck it—let's go!" shouts Joey, as he pulls the door open. "Joey, there was no signal!" Tommy shouts.

"Who is that asshole?!" a pissed off Detective Hawkins asked. Rico looks out his binoculars at Joey, now joined by Tommy, who can't let his partner go in alone.

"That would be Joey Sorvino and Tommy Sato, sir. Another guy gets out of the van. I don't know him," Rico said

"I'll deal with them later! All units—it's a go!" The Task Force and the Asian Gang Unit hit the street— busting out of their vans with automatic weapons and bullet-proof vests.

The men get up to the front door with a door buster. "POLICE!!" The men shout as the door is knocked down. All hell breaks loose as gunfire breaks out inside the mansion. The Yokohama Black Rebels are packing Semi-Automatic weapons and submachine guns, and are shooting at everything that moves. Hadeo puts two men down with a riff from a Mac 10 and runs up the steps with bullets following behind him. "I got two men down over here!" Detective Ozawa shouts on the radio. One rookie Asian officer comes up against a Black Rebel with a Samurai sword and freezes. "Shoot God dammit!" Hawkins ordered. The gangster chops off the rookie's arm just before Hawkins takes him out. The rookie screams in pain. "Which one of these son-of-a-bitches is Hiroshi?!" Washington asked in vain.

"Who knows man?! We'll ask after these bastards are dead!" Thompson answered back. Joey, Tommy and me make our way towards the bedrooms hoping to find Hiroshi—the big prize. I have my gun drawn not looking to use it unless I had to. Joey, on the other hand, brings back memories of him leading the point on a patrol in the jungle.

"Ain't this fun Sammy?!" he asked, with his adrenaline pumping.

"Are you nuts Joey?! We're on the visitor's turf, man. They have home field!" I said. One man jumps out of nowhere ready to fire, but Joey nails him first. Joey looks at me and winks with that devilish smile of his. "Watch out Sam!" Tommy said, pulling me out the way as he shoots down another gangster.

Sweating bullets, I took off my hat and wiped my forehead. Thanks, Tommy," I said as we keep moving down the hall. The gunshots heard throughout the raid coincide with female screams, as the Rebel's girlfriends add to the madness.

"Get down to the secret tunnels!" Hiroshi yelled in Japanese.

We follow the sound of the male voice coming from the end of the hall that you could drive a stretch limo through. We peel up against the wall not to be sitting ducks walking in the middle. We stop just outside the entrance of the last room in the hall as each one of us takes a deep breath. "This is the room guys!" Joey said. "I can feel it in my bones."

"We should wait for back up Joey," Tommy whispered.

"What? Just so that ass-hole Hawkins gets all the glory! Fuck that!"

"You're not John Wayne man, and this ain't Iwo Jima!" Tommy said in anguish. Joey wasn't hearing it. He has that look in his eye—like a man with gold fever or something. Sammy, are you ready to blow the lid off this case?" Joey asked.

"Let's take him down," I said. Just like Tommy said, Joey went in like John Wayne marching up that hill to glory. His gun raised high and without a second thought, Joey fired at anything moving. His target just happened to be a Japanese woman who takes a blast from Joey's pump action shotgun. A man yells—calling out the name Yumi—spraying a round of bullets our way, striking Joey in his vest and upper torso. And Tommy gets it in the shoulder and leg, but to my amazement, I go untouched. I return fire quickly, but the man jumps out the window of the second floor. "TWO OFFICER'S DOWN!!" I yell in Tommy's blood stained radio. I drop the radio and as I drop down to aid Tommy and Joey.

"You okay Tommy?!" I asked. "I'm okay—see to Joey!"
Joey is lying up against a wall, shot multiple times. Joey
has a faint smile on his face as he tries to get up but can't.

"Stay cool Joey—you gonna' be alright, man!"

"Was that him Sammy? Was that Hiroshi?" Joey asked,
gasping for air. I look over at the young lady lying across
the room with her eyes wide open and staring at the
ceiling. "You just hang in there, paison—we'll get him,"
I said. I grab a hold of Joey's hand and hold on tight, just
as we did our brothers in 'Nam.

"I'm sorry…for what I said earlier Sam," Joey said. "I
was a coward. I had a Vietnamese daughter. I didn't
accept her because I was too ashamed. Can you contact
her for me Bro'?" Tommy limps over to us with blood
trailing behind him. "No problem Joey. I'll find her," I
said. Joey coughs up blood while squeezing my hand
harder. "Looks like it's gonna' be pro-bono again my
friend," he said, laughing. "Tommy, get that bastard."

Those were the last words of my friend Joey as the
cavalry comes in. I believe that was Hiroshi that got
away.

Now it's personal for the both of us. He'll get me, or I'll get him before it's all over.

Chapter 46

A big manhunt is launched for Hiroshi's capture and
what's left of his gang for the shooting death of Joey and
two other officers. You kill a cop in this town—you
might as well as shot the President of the United States. It
was a devastating loss to the police department, not to
mention the loss of an old friend. Joey had his faults, but
I believe they were brought on by the lingering effects of
the war. Now to hear that he has a daughter just makes
me sad for her.

While my friend is lying on a slab in the morgue, I head to Connie's place to be with my son. I get greeted at the door from Connie, who was nice enough to make me a hot cup of Joe. "Are you alright?" Connie asked, wearing a night shirt and a warm smile.

"Joey's gone and Tommy's in the hospital," I said softly. I take off my coat and unbuckle my holster and gun, but this time I leave the bullets inside.

Connie lowers her head but stays strong. "I'm sorry Sam." Connie rubs the back of my neck which sure feels good at the moment. I must admit, it sure feels good coming home to a good woman. "Any messages come in for me?"

Two jobs came in," she said with a smile. "A Mrs. Tolliver had a priceless heirloom stolen from her Beverly Hills home and she wants you to find out who took it."

"It's Beverly Hills. The cops there all of a sudden are too busy?" I asked. Connie hands me the note while I take a sip of coffee. "She refused to go to the police.

She wouldn't give me a reason until she talked to you." It's good to get more work. It's like getting a new girlfriend. Once you have a new girlfriend, all the women start coming out of the woodwork. "Looks like you're going to have to hire a new investigator," Connie said.

"Looks like it. What's the other case?" I asked. Connie hands me the message as she yawns.

"It's the usual. A woman wants her cheating husband followed."

"Place an ad for an investigator tomorrow in the L.A. Times, baby." Connie gets a notepad on the counter and writes a message to herself. "Oh, make sure the applicant is not a religious freak. They must be able to handle the seediest of cases," I said. Connie smiles as she finishes the message. "I got it boss."

"What about Saivon?"

"He's sleep. Poor thing was so tired today. We visited several pre-schools," Connie said. "He charmed the staff at all the schools," she gushed.

"That's my boy." We head back to Saivon's room to get a good look at him. I feel bad not being able to spend more time with him. The kid needs me after losing his mom. As we peek in on him, Connie holds my hand. "About the other night Connie…"

"Don't worry about it. We're both single adults. Whatever happens—happens," Connie said, trying not to be too needy.

Chapter 47

To relieve some stress of the case, and to get in the mindset of the Bushido Code, we visit the dojo of Kendo master Taki Akimoto with Armstrong, Ken, and my son. It is also a good time to regroup and be among friends. Master Akimoto has taken the time to have a private workout with us because of the sensitive nature of protecting my client. Kendo is a modern day art of Japanese sword fighting based on Kenjutsu.

The difference of Kendo is that instead of using the actual sword, a wooden sword is used. Saivon tries to pick up a sword that is bigger than his body, and the sword is winning that battle.

Akimoto shows us the importance of footwork as he continually beats us like a drum with one move. Armstrong, at six feet four and awkward in his footwork, gets frustrated and starts to wield his sword like a baseball bat, bringing a smile to Master Akimoto's face.

"You are better suited for Sumo Wrestling!" Master Akimoto said, laughing. We all laugh after that, even Armstrong, whose ashy feet could use some lotion. Ken looks good holding the sword as he and I pair off together. "Saivon, watch your daddy school this young warrior," I said.

"Okay, Daddy!"

"You sure you want your son to see you get embarrassed, old man?" Ken asked.

"Old man?" I asked.

"I just turned thirty-three years old young buck!"

"FIGHT!" The master yelled.

Our sticks smash hard together making a loud whacking sound as we both use the move that Master Akimoto showed us. We both circle around each other looking for an opening with me imitating a Samurai, but failing badly. Even Saivon is laughing hysterically at me.

"Are you two gonna' dance all night or are we gonna' see some fighting?" Armstrong asked.

"All I know is that one move!" I said. Ken unleashes a strike to my shoulder blade just as I lowered my weapon. "WINNER!" Akimoto barked.

"Hey—I wasn't ready," I protested to the master and judge.

"Never take your eyes off your opponent. That is rule number one," Akimoto said as Ken laughs. "Pretty soon, I'll be giving you lessons—old man!" The kid is good—this time. I'll just practice with my stickball bat until I'm ready to get my revenge.

The next day I make a call on Mrs. Lauren Tolliver—a well to do divorcee with a missing heirloom. Going into Beverly Hills, I make it a point to dress for the occasion.

I dress in a charcoal grey double breasted suit with a matching Fedora hat, topped off with my Riviera washed and waxed to the max.

The stares are obvious, but I don't know if it's because I look good or if it's my Black skin. I drive just past Sunset Boulevard and Doheny and make a right to find a row of mansions that would take my whole lifetime to afford. As I pull up to the driveway of a Spanish style home underneath a bevy of palm trees, a butler comes out to meet me.

"Good morning Sir, Mrs. Tolliver is expecting you," he said.

"How do you know who I am?" I asked. The butler looked me up and down with his nose stuck in the air and a voice out of "The Great Gatsby".

"You might say I have a sixth sense about these things Sir."

"Well hell my man, let's take that sixth sense of yours to Vegas—we'd make a killing." The wanna' be English Gent barely cracks a smile as he guides me into a large waiting area that looks like a museum.

"May I take your hat Sir?" he asked. I look around the room with all the fancy statues, and ornaments—things that are beyond my limited knowledge. "No, I'm cool Niles," I said sarcastically.

"That's Harold, Sir. Mrs. Tolliver will be down in a moment. Oh, and I trust you will not touch any of Mrs. Tolliver's pieces."

"Why, of course not Harold." Of course as soon as Harold leaves I couldn't help but to touch the flames, so to speak. Everybody knows you don't tell an inquisitive person not to touch something. It's a very unique collection of art and artifacts from around the world that has to be worth millions. "Those pieces are not the reason you're here Mr. Phillips," Mrs. Tolliver said, walking down a spiral staircase like Gloria Swanson in the movie "Sunset Boulevard".

"Call me Sam please," I said, putting down a small bronze statue.

Mrs. Tolliver seems to look like a woman in her late fifties who's kept herself attractive in the image conscience city of Beverly Hills. No doubt having access to a good plastic surgeon in this town goes a long way. "My husband and I picked that piece up in Mozambique back in 1960," she said proudly. "Where is Mr. Tolliver, Ma'am?" I asked.

"My husband is believed to be dead Sam. His plane went down somewhere in New Guinea about ten years ago. He was an avid adventurer," she said, looking up at a painting of him. "Shall we get down to business?"

As we were head off to handle business, my eyes do a double take as a younger version of Mrs. Tolliver head down the steps looking like a replica of Marilyn Monroe, before she was Marilyn Monroe. You know—the Norma Jean Baker years. "That's my daughter Sidney," Mrs. Tolliver said. Wearing a bikini with a white robe cleverly covering her assets, she walked like a panther without a care in the world.

"Hi Sidney," I said.

"Hi," she answered back. "Mother, I'll be at the pool."

"Please excuse my daughter. She has the manners of a lazy house cat," Mrs. Tolliver said.

Don't worry—I'm just admiring the view, I said to myself.

Chapter 48

After playing fantasy games in my mind with a spoiled
little rich girl, Mrs. Tolliver takes me to a more secluded
area of the place that an outsider like me couldn't find
without a tour guide. Coffee, tea, and finger-food are
waiting on us. The massive room is similar to the last one
we visited except this one has pictures of Mrs. Tolliver
on the set of Hollywood films. A much younger Lauren
Tolliver is standing next to Hollywood icons.

"Is that you standing next to Marilyn Monroe?" I asked.

"Why yes. I used to stand in for Marilyn sometimes
because she would occasionally be late on the set. She
was a beautiful girl."

"You were an actress?" Mrs. Tolliver smiled at my
sudden interest in her. "Once you're an actress honey,
you never stop being one," she said.

"I worked when Hollywood was big! It was the golden years. I worked when this town was run by the Jack Warner and Louis B. Mayer's of the world. Everyone was under contract back then."

"And that's you having drinks with Errol Flynn?" I asked. She touched his face gently with her fingers— looking fondly at him. "He was a notorious playboy, but he always treated you like you were the light of his life."

"Those must have been fun times for you," I said as she begins to reflect on something deeply—maybe on getting old. "It's a cruel reality—getting old in this town as a woman. The only jobs that were offered were picked over first by Betty Davis or Joan Crawford playing bitter old women. I auditioned for "Whatever Happened to Baby Jane", but they, of course, gave it to Betty. After that, all I could get were small television roles.

"That's the place where screen legends go to die!" After watching her little tirade, I pull out a cigarette in hopes that she would change the subject to business.

"What can you tell me about the heirloom that was stolen Mrs. Tolliver?" It doesn't take a doctor to see that bringing up the subject of the heirloom pains this woman. Even the rich can show that they can care about something. "It was a large Emerald stone with hardly any imperfections that my husband found outside the mining area of Columbia," she said.

"How much is the stone worth?" I asked.

"It's priceless!" Mrs. Tolliver reaches into a beautiful desk's drawer and pulls out a picture and hands it to me. "It's a picture of the emerald stone. See the richness of the color. And the clarity is flawless."

"It's a beautiful stone Ma'am," I said. "Again I ask, why haven't you told the police Mrs. Tolliver?"

"Please—call me Lauren." Lauren paces around the room, seeming a little rattled when I mentioned the police—a familiar look in my old neighborhood. But here in Beverly Hills, that look is usually associated with child molesters and arsonists. "If I tell you, you must keep this between us…"

"It says it on my office door—Private Ma'am." Mrs. Tolliver pulls out some fancy cigarettes from her desk but can't light it because her lighter won't work. I quickly pull out my lighter and hold it up to her cigarette. "Are you always this helpful?" she asked as she calms down. "Oh, I can be a Black Superman Lauren—always there when you need me," I said smiling. I can tell I was starting to win her over because of the way she was loosening up to me. She drags on a cigarette like it's the last cigarette on Earth, savoring each puff.

"I can't go to the police because my husband didn't report the discovery to the Columbian Government about the Emerald stone," Mrs. Tolliver acknowledged. That was Mr. Tolliver's first mistake. Stealing a poor country's resources is the quickest way to a string of bad luck. "What would you say is the value of the stone necklace Mrs. Tolliver?" I asked. "About 1.5 million dollars," Mrs. Tolliver said, like it was just dinner conversation with her rich friends. I almost break the lead off my pencil after hearing that little gem, no pun intended.

It makes me wonder even more why this extremely rich socialite wants to use me to find her necklace. "1.5 million dollars is a lot of money Mrs. Tolliver."

"And I'm willing to pay you top dollar to recover it Sam," she said. Recover she said. I'm still trying to recover from that bombshell she just laid on me. "Okay…Lauren. I'll take five thousand up front with three hundred dollars a day for expenses." She smiles gently as she goes to her desk again. "I was willing to pay you ten thousand up front and five hundred dollars a day in expenses," she said.

"My old man told me never to argue with a woman because it's an exercise in futility. So, I'll take that rate Ma'am—just to make you happy." Lauren happily writes me a check and hands me a piece of paper with a list of names. "That's a list of names of all the people who were at a small party that I gave the night my necklace was stolen." I fold up the paper and put it inside my suit coat inside pocket. "I'll be in touch Lauren," I said, calmly leaving.

I walk back to my car still reeling and a fat check for ten thousand dollars burning a hole in my pocket. I open the glove compartment to pull out a cigar. As I light the stogie, I lean back to adsorb getting this job like I just won the lottery.

Chapter 49

After celebrating with Connie over getting our most
lucrative case, we go to pick up Saivon, who's at
Kindergarten school for his first day. As he walks back to
the car with Connie, I detect a not so happy look on his
face. "What's the matter Son?" I asked.

"His teacher said he got into a fight," Connie said.
My eyebrows rise in shock as Saivon scoots all the way
to the back of the back seat. "They made fun of me," the
emotional kid said. "Did you kick their ass?" He smiles
for a moment, but Connie shakes her head in disbelief. "I
can't believe you asked him that. This behavior is what
happens when you take him to martial art classes."
Connie said. I laugh as I remember how fun that class
was. Now I know the kid can benefit from taking a few
classes.

"What's so funny?" Connie asked.

"Connie, every boy goes through this in Kindergarten. The boys are trying to establish who the alpha male is that's all," I said.

They said I looked funny," Saivon uttered. His lack of the language calls for some street lingo that Saivon needs to get accustomed with if he's going to make it out here. "Son, you just tell them—Yo' Momma!"

"Your Mommy!" Saivon shouts. I laugh so hard I almost lose control of the car.

"No son. It's yo' Momma!"

"Yo' Momma!" Even Connie had to laugh that time.

"Now you've got to add some hot sauce to it. Say, yo' Momma—sucka'!"

"Yo' Momma, sucka'!" The kid is a natural. He ain't taking no jive from nobody. We laughed out loud all the way home, cracking jokes at each other along the way.

Tommy is hold up under police protection in the hospital's Intensive Care Unit. Every since the shooting he's been under constant watch by the police department.

A uniformed officer sits outside Tommy's room. Inside the room, Tommy is heavily sedated with pain medication. A nurse has just checked on his vitals and left. Coming down the hall is a Japanese uniformed officer looking at the room numbers. It's Hiroshi, disguising himself as a cop. A nurse is heading towards Hiroshi—the same nurse that just came out of Tommy's room. "Excuse me nurse. Where is Room 219?" Hiroshi asked.

"You go down the hall and make a right—it's the first room on the right," she said.

"Thank you very much," Hiroshi answered back with a smile. Hiroshi follows the nurse's directions and head down the hall with total confidence. His smile turns to a look of a man who wants to make the world pay for what's happened to his girlfriend and half his men at that house. Hiroshi gets just pass the corner and finds an officer seated outside Tommy's room. He hesitates for a moment and then continues on his mission.

"What are you doing here—there's still 30 minutes left on my shift?" the officer asked.

"Tommy was a friend of mine. I owe him my life partner. I just want to pay him back you know." The officer thinks for a moment until Hiroshi reaches in his pocket and pulls out a wad of cash. "Here—have some coffee and donuts on me," Hiroshi said.

"Alright man!" The officer looks around and then takes off like a bat out of hell down the hall. Hiroshi calmly walks into Tommy's room to see a helpless Tommy asleep. He reaches in his pocket and pulls out a suppressor for his pistol.

He twists it on carefully—focused on Bushido—the warrior's way. He points the gun at Tommy and utters in Japanese to Tommy. "This is for Sachiko." He pumps two bullets into Tommy and kills him. The EKG Monitor goes off—flat lining. Hiroshi quickly leaves the room with his revenge served frosty cold.

Chapter 50

Connie, Saivon, and I arrive at Connie's place to
Armstrong waiting on us. The nervous look on his face
tells me it can't be good news. "Did you hear the news
Sam?!" Armstrong asked. We barely got out of the car
when Armstrong asked that question, a departure from
his usual demeanor. "What news, man? Is it about Joey's
funeral?"

"No, brother! They got to Tommy inside the hospital.
He's dead!" Armstrong said.

"Come inside Armstrong. I'll have Connie take
Saivon," I said. My two closest friends at the precinct are
now gone, and I'm pretty sure it was Hiroshi who killed
Tommy in revenge. According to Armstrong, witnesses
reported seeing an Asian cop walking away from
Tommy's room. "You were the only other person in that
room that day," said Armstrong.

"You can bet your ass that this motha' fucka' is coming for you, Boss. It's time to bring in a little help." Armstrong gives me that look of his—the one that he does when he's about to tell me something outrageous. You know, like telling me he saw King Kong walking down the middle of Hollywood Boulevard, only to find out he was jiving me about a man in a monkey suit.

"Who did you have in mind 'Strong?" I asked.

"Willie Walker."

"You mean "Crazy" Willie Walker?!" I asked in amazement. "Armstrong—what the hell are you thinking man? Mr. Double agent—Willie Walker would sell us out to the highest bidder." Willie Walker at one time was the biggest snitch in Los Angeles. When they made Starsky and Hutch the television show, the character Huggy Bear was taken from Willie. Shit, he's still probably asking for his cut. "Now I know you two had a big disagreement the last time he worked for you…"

"I brought him in to do a job for my father before I went in the service, and that fool turned around and sold private information to other Private Dicks. My father lost two big clients! Is that a big enough disagreement for you!?"

"So is that a yes or no?" Armstrong asked. "He's a changed man Sam. He was the best you know."

"What's your connection to all this 'Strong? You seem mighty anxious to have him come in," I said. I hand Armstrong a beer and he rips open the can and downs a gulp so fast it spills down his shirt. "The fool married my sister while you were in the service. She wants him to get out and do something." I laugh so hard I almost forgot what we needed him for in the first place. "He's driving my sister crazy man, and then she tells me every detail of their marriage life," Armstrong said, looking as if he's about to lose it. I can't afford to have my right hand man going "One Flew Over the Cuckoo's Nest" on me
when I need him the most.

"You should have told me 'Strong…'"

"I know…I know Sam! Can you do it?"

"All I can do is promise to talk to him," I said.

And that's exactly what we did. I met Crazy Willie for the first time in six years. Marriage life has added a few pounds to his five foot seven inch frame. Armstrong came along also to act as referee. "What's up Willie?" I asked, extending my hand.

"It's my main man Sam!" Willie shouts, grabbing me in a bear hug. "What's shakin' baby?! I haven't seen you since…"

"Since you fucked over my father's trust back in '70." Willie has an embarrassed look on his face that is surprising compared to the guy I knew back when. "I'm sorry about that Sam. Your father was a good man, and I was a different cat back then," Willie said.

"Why should I trust you, "Crazy" Willie?" Willie pulls out a little black book and shows it to me.

"I know you just a big job in Beverly Hills, Boss," he said. The first thing I did was look over at Armstrong. "Armstrong could have told you that news," I said.

"I never tell anyone about our cases man."

"You think Armstrong would have told me that?" Willie's got a point there. He was known as having the biggest mouth in the West.

"Okay, I'll give you a shot. But if you screw me, I'm coming after you Willie."

Chapter 51

Joey and Tommy are laid to rest in front of fellow officers, friends, and family. A gun salute sounds off, firing up a tense crowd. It's a big burial crowd as police from every precinct is there. The mayor is also in attendance along with the police chief, and Captain Pierpont. The other Asian Crime Unit is there as Maria Ozawa, Charles Thompson, and Fred "Downtown" Washington, look on as the shots go off in the quiet morning.

It's tough seeing my two friends get laid to rest knowing that I was just with them only a couple of days ago. Joey and I didn't see eye to eye in our last days together, but we both shared a bond that was unbreakable. Connie is with me also while Saivon is at school.

It's the beginning of September as a nice breeze circulates throughout the crowd. I think about that moment inside the big mansion that day and wonder if I could have done anything different. The moment plays over and over like a tape being rewind and fast forwarded again. Whatever I do, it doesn't change a damn thing. Joey and Tommy are gone, and that bastard Hiroshi is still out there.

Hadeo and some of his men are holding someone in an abandoned building in Little Tokyo, the result of businesses leaving because of gangster's strong-arming their way inside.

The man they're holding is Koichi Nakamura, a local businessman that informed on Hiroshi to the police. Already bloodied and battered like a chop steak beaten with a spiked hammer, Hiroshi pleads for his life. "Please…you have the wrong guy! I would never inform on Mr. Ito!" Koichi pleads.

"You are a snitch Nakamura! Now someone has snitched on you!" Hadeo said laughing.

"Please, I have a family! I have kids!"

"We will take good care of them!" shouts one gangster. Hiroshi arrives in the building with his bodyguards around him. Everyone greets Hiroshi with a traditional Japanese gesture of respect. Hiroshi calmly walks over to Koichi who by this time is wetting in his pants. Hiroshi's steely gaze strikes fear in the eyes of men. He doesn't need to talk much if he didn't want to. Hiroshi has been on a recruiting mission. Not being able to bring fresh men from Japan fast enough, he's hired local friends of his associates. Some of the men are not the sharpest tools in the shed, and he knows it. "Hadeo, is this the bastard that snitched on me?" Hiroshi asked.

"This is he. He's not much of a man—he's soiled his pants!"

"Twice!" one gangster jokes. Hiroshi grabs Koichi by the face and twists it to one side to the other. "You've cost me a lot of pain and money," Hiroshi said with his sadistic side starting to come through. On a table sits a variety of "tools" for Hiroshi to use at his disposal. Hiroshi looks over at the table, and Koichi follows Hiroshi's eyes over to the table.

"I can be of assistance to you!" Koichi pleads. "I can inform you of the other merchants that may be cheating you or other things."

"That's not a bad idea. I can use someone on the inside." Koichi is relieved for a moment. "However, I will lose face if I don't take something from you," Hiroshi said. "The Yakuza takes fingers. What should I take from you?" Koichi again starts to sweat like a pig being slaughtered. "Uh—two fingers?" The sadistic gangsters all laugh.

"We're not Yakuza you fool!" Hadeo said.

"I can't take your legs because you have to be able to walk around to talk to the other merchants," Hiroshi said. Koichi shakes his head in agreement. Hiroshi suddenly looks at Koichi's arm. "Hold your arm out."

Koichi is too slow to move. "No—please no!" A couple of henchmen pulls Koichi's arm out for him as he screams. Hadeo hands Hiroshi a gleaming Katana Samurai sword. "This won't hurt a bit!" Koichi turns his head to Hiroshi and instead gets two bullets from a .45 automatic with a suppressor into his forehead. "Hiroshi cries out for bushido!" His henchmen place Koichi's body in a big plastic sheet. "I WANT THAT P.I.!!!

Part Four   Get Sam

Chapter 52

I got a call from Mrs. Tolliver's daughter Sidney who told me her mother wanted to see me. The message told me to come around to the pool area in the back. I pull up to the driveway, and the butler is not here to greet me. Reluctantly I leave the Riviera parked on the inside of the driveway just in case some jive turkey doesn't get an idea. I straighten my tie and put on my suit coat just before I take a quick look around. My father always told me to look around to see what's going on around your surroundings. "Never let anyone creep up behind you," he'd always say.

I head towards the back hoping to see a friendly face or two. Maybe there's a party going on, and I'm the first to arrive. Anything is possible I guess.

To my surprise the only person I see is the person who left the message with Connie. That person is Sidney, whose swimming nude in the gigantic pool. Talk about looking around your surroundings. My head turns three hundred and sixty degrees around just like Linda Blair in the Exorcist. "Come on in—the water's great!" Sidney blurts out.

"No—it's safer over here," I answered back. Sidney swims toward me as I keep looking around for someone to rescue me. "Is your mom at home?"

"No—she left town on business," Sidney said, smiling. I feel like a little bird about to be swallowed by a cat. "Your message said your mom had important information for me, Sidney." She giggles at me like she's smacking me around with her paws. "I lied," she said.

"You're a very dangerous girl Sidney," I said, loosening up my tie in the heat.

"Don't you forget it Sam," a smiling Sidney said.

"Oh, I won't. It's not every day a Black man gets invited to a private pool party in Beverly Hills with a naked White girl." Somehow I believe this is not Sidney's first rodeo at raging against the machine.

"I saw the way you looked at me the other day," she said, holding on to the edge of the pool. "I'm a man baby. I was born to look at women." I stoop down and stick my hand in the water just to feel the cool liquid between my fingers. "See—I told you the water's nice," Sidney said.

"Where's that stuffy butler of yours—don't tell me he left town on business too?"

"No—I gave him the day off, silly."

"Sidney, I'm a very busy man. And with gas the way it is, I've burned away at least five dollars of it," I said. Hell, five dollars means nothing to Sidney. She'll probably never have to worry about doing an honest day's work in her life. Her mother will do everything she can to keep Sidney living the way she's accustomed to.

"What do I have to do to keep you from investigating this case?" she asked while caressing my ankle.

"Now why would you want me to drop your mother's case?" I asked.

"Could you be a dear and get me a towel please?" I retrieve a towel and hold it up for Sidney as she climbs out of the pool. "Thank you," she said with a touch of coyness.

She strolls over to the lounge chair with that walk that she's patented. All I could do is take my hat off and wipe my sweaty forehead. "My mother has done this sort of thing before in the past. My father's gone, so she creates these big events to make her feel important. It's embarrassing. My brother and I have to put up with it all the time."

"I didn't know you have a brother," I said.

"His name is Ryan. He's away at school," Sidney said while taking off her swim cap to release her head full of blonde locks. "Still—your mother gave me a lot of money to investigate this, little lady so…" Sidney gets up from the chair and throws her arms around me that almost knock the wind out of me from the impact.

"Wouldn't you want to have me instead of that money?!" she asked. I feel like I'm on an episode of "Let's make a Deal" and audience members are screaming both ways—take the girl, or take the money. Before I could say anything, Sidney kisses me full on the mouth and holds it for what seems like a Guinness Book world record. "You have soft lips," she said.

"Yes—I get that a lot. Women tell me all the time about my lips. It's a blessing and a curse. Gotta' go Sidney. I have a case to solve." And with that I was on my way before nosy neighbors could get me caught up with something I couldn't get out of.

Chapter 53

I found out from Det. Charles Thompson that Koichi was
pulled from the ocean today, so I was summoned to
Captain Pierpont's office. Moral is at an all time low in
the office as everyone is still grieving for Joey and
Tommy. Even Ramona is a little nicer to me than the last
time I've seen her. "How's your son doing Sam?" she
asked softly.

"He's a great kid. He's doing great," I said. Ramona is
continuously looking in her purse for nothing in
particular it seems. At the moment, there are no calls, so
she's just trying to look busy. "Joey told me you two
were…seeing each other."

"He did?!"

"Oh yeah, man for sure. He told me he was really
digging on you, and that he always did." That seems to
have lifted Ramona's spirit.

She always wanted to be the center of a man's world. "Thank you Sam for saying that," she said.

"He seemed happy that last day, baby. I think you two would have had something there."

"That means a lot coming from you Sam." Pierpont comes out and waves me in without barking at me first. I don't know if I could handle a softer, gentler Pierpont. It would throw the balance of the world off if you can dig that. Sitting in the office is Charlie and Detective Maria Ozawa. "Sit down Phillips, we were just going over something that I think you should hear," Pierpont said.

"What's up Captain?"

"I know that you and Joey were good friends to the point of me seeing you a little too much around the precinct. Now that Joey and Tommy are gone I've instructed Thompson, and Ozawa here to keep you informed of any cases that we might be too busy to handle," the captain said, biting his lip. "Well, Captain, I appreciate you keeping me in the loop. And I will keep you also informed," I said.

It was a Kodak moment for us. Joey and Tommy were a big presence in the precinct and was the top team of the Asian Crime Unit. The captain clears his throat after the emotional moment as Ozawa wipes a tear. "I guess you heard about our informant getting fished out of the ocean this morning," Pierpont said. "What you don't know is that before he was killed, Kiochi told us the whereabouts of some of Hiroshi's businesses. Tomorrow we're going to hit him hard where it counts—in his wallet."

"If we take out some of Hiroshi's businesses, the community won't fear him as much and will begin to rise against him. At least that what we're counting on," Maria said.

"Count me in," I insisted.

I left the precinct in good spirits, knowing that I have a new relationship with the captain. A good P.I. needs access to the local department for records and other stuff

I figure it's time to earn my money as I check out the first person on Mrs. Tolliver's hit list. Edward Steinberg, a rich movie producer who lives in the Hollywood Hills, is first on my list.

According to Mrs. Tolliver, Mr. Steinberg is known as the B-version of "The King of the B- movies. A title he says was taken from him by Roger Corman. Mrs. Tolliver said Steinberg showed the most interest in the Emerald piece.

"I drive up the winding streets up through the hills reaching almost the top to find Steinberg's decked out pad. Looking like something out of the Jetson's with its futuristic style, this cat's crib must hold some bodacious parties. Unlike Mrs. Tolliver, Mr. Steinberg greets me without the need of a butler or a maid—strange for the area.

"Mr. Steinberg—Sam Phillips sir," I said, giving him my card. Steinberg looks at my card and immediately has a curious look on his face. "What can I do for you Mr. Phillips?"

"Please—call me Sam sir. Steinberg waves me in the house wearing casual clothing with sandals and his hair slicked back in grey ponytail that gives me the impression that he's somewhat of a hippie. Two small dogs arrive suddenly—smelling at my feet. Two white poodles that look like "show dogs".

"That's Brutus, and the other one is Lucy," he said. "My other half is sleeping right now, so we have to keep the conversation low."

"I'm investigating an Emerald necklace that's missing from Lauren Tolliver's place. She said you were one of her guests at the party she gave." Steinberg chuckles a bit as he remembers that night. I remember that night. Lauren showed that big outlandish stone to the whole party for some crazy reason. It was obviously absurdly expensive. Who'd do such a thing in this day and time? Look around you, Mr. Phillips. That necklace is definitely not my taste." I look around just as he asked, and he's right—the necklace doesn't fit the style.

"That doesn't mean you couldn't walk out with the stone and sell it to some other high roller to keep you living in this luxury for the rest of your life," I said. Steinberg laughs again at my notion as he sips on Perrier Water. "Mr. Phillips, my dear good man. My movies have generated over two hundred million dollars worldwide with five more movies in the can. I'm already living the life of luxury," he answered back.

"Touché, Sir."

"Is there anything else I can do for you, Mr. Phillips?" Steinberg asked.

"How about a part in one of them movies of yours," I said, joking. Steinberg, taking a quick walk around me for sport I suspect. "You know…I do see a cross between John Shaft and Mister Tibbs in you," he said. He quickly walks over to a desk in the den and hands me his business card too. "Why don't you come over to Paramount tomorrow and see me on the set. You could be just what I'm looking for."

"Oh no… I was just joking around—"

"Nonsense! You're perfect," he insisted. I stopped Steinberg just short of getting "too" Hollywood friendly— you know…calling me baby and shit. "Right now I have too many things on the plate my man. A man needs to know his limitations in life." I walk out not getting closer to the Emerald necklace, but a legitimate offer for a movie role. Can you dig it?

Chapter 54

I've taken Saivon to his grandmother's place so that
Connie and me can get some alone time together. She's
worked hard taking care of my son while also handling
the business as well. By showing my appreciation, I've
cooked a home cooked meal for the first time since I can
remember. Ramona and I never made time for having
home cooked meals if you know what I mean. I prepared
a pasta dish of Linguini with chopped lobster and chicken
breast and white fettuccine sauce, fresh garlic and virgin
olive oil. To top it off I made smothered lamb to die for,
and a nice red wine to wash it down. I learned to cook
this from the best—my mother of course.

Connie has never seen this side of me; so of course,
she's blown away by the big spread. "Wow, you went all
out, huh boss?!" she asked.

"I'm only boss at the office baby. Here we're just Sam and Connie. Connie tasted a sample of the pasta with a big fork. Her reaction said it all as she nearly dropped to the floor it was so good. "The garlic cheese bread is in the oven," I said. I have fresh flowers on the table followed by the stereo playing Barry White. You can't get any better than that.

"I'm digging this side of you Sam Phillips. What do you have in mind for dessert?"

"Hey—I'm an expert at keeping things a secret sweetheart," I joked.

"Oh, I forgot—excuse me," Connie said. I didn't want to go into the real reason I was cooking this great dinner for her. I didn't tell her about me going in on another raid with the police. A raid that left my two friends killed. I know she'd try to talk me out of it. After all, I'm a Private Dick, not a cop. Tomorrow goes unmentioned, as we laughed, drank wine, and made love until we knocked ourselves out from exhaustion.

The next morning I arrived at the precinct just after role call started. The sergeant has done his best to convince everyone of the magnitude of the job ahead.

"We all have a job to do," the sergeant said. "This is the man that's responsible for taking the lives of two of our own. Let's turn his world upside down, and let him know—he's fucked with the wrong people! Let's be careful out there! Go get him!" The room is full of fired up cops and detectives. It's something they needed to get off their chests. "Sam—you're riding with me!" Fred Washington shouted out. We get to Fred's patrol car, and when he opens up the trunk, it looks as though he robbed an armory. "What you Fred—win some free coupons at the gun store?" I asked.

"Here—put this on," he responded, handing me a bullet proof vest. "I guess until they find me a partner, you're it." I looked at the pump action shotgun and had to pick it up and hold it. "No, this is it for me. Exchanging information is one thing, but going on raids…there's just too many bullets flying around you dig?" Fred gets a big laugh out of that comment. Fred grew up in Watts and was a rookie on the force when the riots happened in '65. He's seen a lot over the years and does not rattle easily. "You were in 'Nam brother. This shit should be a cake walk for you."

"Yea—I was in that jungle, and I'm paying the price by taking drugs every day."

"I hear that."

Chapter 55

Hiroshi's clubs were first on the hit list, as we bust through the bouncers that set off an avalanche of ass busting and head knocking fights. Ozawa is truly in her elements as she kicks men's ass much bigger than her. A guy cold cocks me that sent me over a table backwards. I must admit it felt good. I haven't been in a bar fight in a long time.

Washington gets payback on the guy by hitting him with the butt of his gun. He then helps me up off the beer drenched floor as the raid escalates. Suddenly, shots are fired from some gangsters that lead to the Gang Unit to return fire.

We head towards the back of the building as prostitutes and "Johns" pour out from the back in droves. It's hard to tell if the "Johns" aren't really gangsters trying to run out with the crowd, so the police are arresting everyone.

Everyone is looking to notch Hiroshi on their gun, but there's no sign of him. "Hiroshi! Hiroshi!" a detective shots to a gangster.

"Fuck you—Pig!!" the man said. For his choice of words, the young bad ass gets a club upside the head. Pierpont joins the melee looking to relive his old days of cracking heads on the mean L.A. Streets. "See, Phillips— they're nothing but a bunch of young punks!" Pierpont said, sticking his chest out as the crowd is being rustled up like cattle. Suddenly from out of nowhere, a masked gunman surprises everyone especially Captain Pierpont, who the gunman has his sights on.

"Yokohama Black Rebels!!" the man yells as he pulls his gun. Knocking Pierpont out of the way, I pull my trusty .45 and shoot the hoodlum in the chest. Charles and Maria pounce on the wounded gangster and quickly pick up his gun. I help up a rattled Captain Pierpont up from the floor sporting a cut lip. I receive pats on the back from the unit, and a strange, heartfelt handshake from a man who has belittled me for over a year now. The man's scowl rivals that of "Dirty Harry".

"I guess I owe you my life, Phillips," Pierpont said, humbled. His gruff manner is still intact, but less Scrooge-like. "You can thank me by buying me a cold one—if we get out of this alive!" I said. The room that the hoodlum rushed out of is stormed in by everyone.

"POLICE!! Get your hands up!" the police shouted at several gang members give up. A frantic search pursues to see if Hiroshi is one of the men inside. A look around the large room displays a sordid and deranged mind of a sadistic man. There are chains, whips, naked women and men. Not to mention, perverse looking statues of sexual deviance going on. Some of the Gang Unit laughs as they handcuff the Rebels. "Man, what a whack job!" some joked.

"Unfortunately, a lot of Japanese men are sexually perverted," Ozawa said.

"You think?" Thompson laughed. Washington picks up a statue and gives it a once over.

"Maybe we can take some of these items in for evidence, hey Captain." Pierpont goes up to one of the Black Rebels and slaps him. "Where is Hiroshi?!" he snaps. The Black Rebel gangster laughs in Pierpont's face. He then looks over at me with a crooked smile—the kind of smile you give when you just picked someone's pocket.

"Are you…Sam Phillips?" he asked.

"I'm Sam. Who wants to know?" I asked.

"I'm looking at a dead man," the punk said. I walk up to the young punk and put my last business card in his shirt pocket. "I want you to hear this from me so there won't be no jive talkin' punk. You tell Hiroshi I'll be waiting for him. Can you remember that? If not, here's a little help." I slug the little creep in the stomach that leaves him gasping on the floor.

Chapter 56

I figured it was time I had a little meeting with Johnny—Michelle's boyfriend, so I bring Armstrong with me to scare him straight. I figured it was Johnny who ratted us out to Hiroshi a few weeks ago. As we drive down the 101 Freeway, Armstrong feels this is the right moment to ask for a more prominent role in my business.

"That Ken is a good kid, hey Sam?" Armstrong asked. "The kid's cool. He just needed some strong male role models in his life," I said. Armstrong is squirming like a man in a dentist chair as he tries to get to the point.

"I think I've been a responsible dude in protecting the young blood."

"You've been my rock big guy."

"I think it's time for me to get my P.I.'s license," Armstrong said. Now that Armstrong has gotten it off his chest, he sighs and puts the ball in my court. "I think you're right Armstrong. You've made your bones my brother," I said, smiling. Armstrong as expected is shocked by my answer. "So does this mean you'll back me in getting my license?"

"Well, first you have to go through all the paperwork first. And then there is the matter of your arrest," I said. "But I think saving the police captain's life warrants a few favors."

"Right on, man!"

It was Crazy Willie who gave us the information on the whereabouts on Johnny. That little peanut head hustler came through. He also told me there's a price on my head courtesy of the Yokohama Black Rebels for ten thousand dollars. Inflation doesn't get you much these days. I'm worth a hell of a lot more than that. "Are you okay back there Johnny?!" I asked.

A loud thump comes from the back of the car. Armstrong laughs as Johnny pleads for his life in the trunk of my car.

"Now you didn't think we've forgotten about you settin' us up did you?!"

"I was forced to do it! They were going to kill my family!" Johnny screamed.

"Good! Then help me help you Johnny! Tell us where we can find Hiroshi!" We drive Johnny to some abandoned docks in the downtown area, north of Chinatown. Armstrong opens up the trunk and pulls Johnny out shaking out of pure fear. "Where are we?!" Johnny asked. "This is the place where they're going to find you ten years from now, buried underneath bricks and wood sucka'!" Armstrong said. We drag Johnny inside kicking and screaming until we found the perfect spot to interrogate him. "Leave him with me boss, I'll make him talk," Armstrong said. "I don't like his punk ass anyhow!" I hold Armstrong off like a rabid dog, just enough that he can feel Armstrong's massive grip.

"You better talk or I'll let my man start breaking something Johnny!"

"I don't know where Hiroshi hangs! I've only been to the Rising Sun Nightclub! Please—I don't want to die!" Armstrong grabs Johnny by the neck and tries to twist it off.

"Be easy big fella'. I believe the piece of shit. Hiroshi has been one step ahead of everybody. He wouldn't talk loose around Johnny." Armstrong releases Johnny but is none too happy about it. "You gotta' let me hit something sometime boss. You gotta' let me out of the cage dammit!

"Stay away from Michelle, Johnny. She and Ken are under my protection. Go back to making crappy movies—smoke pot and cocaine exactly like every other director in Hollywood. If you don't, this will be your burial ground—dig it?"

Johnny got the message. He tore out of there like Tony Dorsett—never looking back.

Chapter 57

I unleashed Armstrong from his cage, just like he wanted alright. I unleashed him onto Little Tokyo like Godzilla smashing little buildings, like Samson killing the Philistines with the jaw bone of a mule. He wreaked havoc and unleashed a reign of terror on the bad guys in the community he could have run for mayor—and won.

He was a one man wrecking crew, and he loved it. With the blessing of the Asian Gang Unit, Little Tokyo wasn't ready for a badass like Armstrong Jones. He and his gun are leaving a trail of bad guys along the way.

With Hiroshi on the run, the merchants are now emboldened to come out from the shadows.

Armstrong has also sampled from the lovely Asian locals as well, sometimes two or three at a time. "Mr. Armstrong, are you sure you can handle all three of us?" one girl asked.

"Momma-san, when I'm through with you, you're going to be callin' home to Japan to tell your daddy what they say is not a myth."

With Armstrong's bold tactics, his actions have created the opening the Asian Gang Unit was looking for. They arrest any remaining Black Rebels courtesy of tips from local merchants. There is still no arrest of Hiroshi and Hadeo, which still has the community on guard.

Being on a hit list has pissed me off. I take it personal, and when I take it personal I don't run and cower—I lock and load. With Saivon enjoying his time with his new granny, I make time with Connie to go over a few options.

I make it to the apartment to find Connie watching television on the couch, and eating take-out. "Is this what I pay you for—to sit down during the day and watch soap operas?" I asked. "Which one is it this time—Ryan's Hope, Search for Tomorrow?"

"It's All My Children—and I'm taking my break, just like I was in the office," Connie said. I take a look at my watch and realize that it's noon. Connie looks up at me with a sarcastic look before diving back into her soap. "Okay, I might have jumped the gun a little." Connie turns off the TV set and hands me a message. "Lauren Tolliver called. She's back in town and wants to meet with you," she said. I read the message anyway and then put it away in my pocket. I have more important issues to discuss with Connie. "Can you turn off the TV Connie, I have something important to lay on you," I said. Connie doesn't hear me because of the distraction of her favorite show. I reached around and turned off the set that definitely got Connie's attention. "You just turned off Erica Kane!"

I pull Connie up from the couch by her arm—caveman style to show her who's the boss. Instead, all Connie could was smile, but it was a smile of seduction. She enjoyed the physicality.

"Okay—it's not that kind of party Little Momma," I said. I reached around my back and pulled out my .32 caliber back up piece. I unload the bullets and place them on the table. "I'm giving you this gun for protection."

"You want me with a gun?" Connie asked, stunned. "I've never used a gun in my life!" I put the gun in her hand so that she could get a feel. "It's sexy huh?" I asked.

"Why am I doing this?" Connie asked curiously.

"I'm on a hit list, so that means that anyone who's associated with me could get hurt. I'd prefer you to take a vacation," I said. Connie gets a more determined look on her face. She may look like a classic Librarian, but underneath she's Wonder Woman. "So, what do I now?" she asked, holding the gun tighter. "You aim the weapon and squeeze the trigger." Connie squeezes one off like a natural. She digs it, so she does it over and over again.

"When can I shoot the real thing? I want to hit something."

"Take it easy, Annie Oakley. You got somebody you're looking to take out soon?" I take the gun out of her hand and load the shells. "This is how you load the gun. Be careful now—she's sensitive," I said. Connie repeats what I've done until she gets good at it. "I'd feel a lot better if you'd take a leave Connie."

"You're a P.I. Sam. Some of your cases are dangerous. I knew that when I signed up. I'm hooked now. You're stuck with me."

Chapter 58

With the Yokohama Black Rebels all but run out of town, I can just about close the case on Michelle and Ken. But first I have one case still open that's paying the bills, so I thought I'd better go out to Beverly Hills to meet with Mrs. Tolliver to give her an update. It was something that her daughter Sidney had said that stuck with me. She said that her mother was just doing this for publicity. It wouldn't be the first time a has-been screen legend has sought publicity to put themselves in the limelight again. It's a cruel town, and like my father said, "If you're not the best at what you do, don't come out here because this town will swallow you whole."

I was let in by Harold, who is still as stiff as Lurch on the Addams Family. "How's it hangin' Harold? I know you missed me right?"

"I beg your pardon sir?" Harold asked. There's still no warm and fuzziness from Harold. He walks me through the mausoleum of a home that has to be the place to be at Halloween. Harold takes me through the house, as I was looking to see Lauren by now. He takes me out to the tennis court where Lauren and Sidney are playing tennis with two young, male tennis guides. Lauren and Sidney were playing against each other—a doubles match in particular.

"Sam!" Lauren shouts out. Lauren heads toward me as Sidney continues playing with her coach. "Is that the man you were talking about?" the coach said to Sidney.

"Yes, that's him. Tall, dark, and dark," Sidney said with a smirk.

"He doesn't look that tough," the coach said. Sidney tosses the tennis ball at her coach.

"Shut up and serve." Lauren towels herself off and takes a sip of a cool drink that Harold has brought to her

"You play tennis Sam?" she asked.

"No, where I grew up there were no tennis courts," I said, smiling.

"Oh and where did you grow up?"

"I'm from St. Louis originally. The only recreation we had was stick ball, baseball, and basketball. If we wanted to go swimming, we turned on the fire hydrants." The things I'm talking about seem alien to Lauren. She looks at me as though she was staring at a Norman Rockwell painting. "Oh, I see," she said. "I'd like to hear about the case. Let's go inside." We go inside where Harold has prepared finger foods—a nice spread at that. "I hope you don't mind—have you eaten?" she asked.

"I'm sure I can make room," I joked. I give my hat to Harold and sit down at the table. Lauren is being courteous, maybe too courteous. I feel like I'm being fattened up for something I might regret. "I don't know how welcomed I'm going to be once you've heard what I've got Mrs. Tolliver, which is nothing. I've talked to some of your friends who are accusing you of seeking publicity for a big comeback—including Sidney," I said. For some reason, the lady doesn't seem shocked by her friend's reactions.

"My daughter thinks I'm seeking publicity?"

"Are you—seeking publicity? I mean it's cool with me—it's your money."

"Yes I would like to come back to acting, but my precious necklace is missing Sam," Lauren said. I'm starting to believe her. There are better ways to get publicity as a woman in her position. Sidney walks in still dressed in her outfit and her young coach in tow. "Sam, you remember Sidney. I want you to meet her friend Chad," Lauren said. I nod at Chad as he sizes me up—for what I don't know. "Do you carry a gun?" Chad asked.

"Don't be silly Chad. Of course, he does. Look at the bulge in his pants," Sidney said.

"I'm sure that's not where he carries his gun." I could nothing but laugh inside at the two of them. You take away the silver spoon in their mouths, and they would be drowning in their ignorance. "Yes I do carry a gun, and its big kids." I turn my attention toward Lauren again as I can see that she's somehow envious of her daughter's youthful appearance. "Should we continue this in private, Mrs. Tolliver?" I asked.

234

"There are no secrets with Mother and me, Sam. Isn't that right Mother? We share everything. And I mean…everything," Sidney said provocatively. Sidney picks up a finger food and stuffs in her mouth, all the while laughing at Lauren. Sidney's actions of course have struck a nerve in Lauren. She calmly gets up from her chair, walks over to Sidney and promptly slaps the taste out of Sidney's mouth.

"Sam please excuse my daughter's behavior. We can finish up in my study." We finished up for the day alright. Lauren gave me the confidence to continue on with the case no matter how ugly things may get, or how expensive. It's a sentimental journey for her she said. It was a time in her life that she was very happy—and that's saying something.

Chapter 59

It's been weeks since Hiroshi has been seen. The police have all but given up looking for the elusive killer. I make it to the office for the first time in a while as Miss Bernice is there to greet me. Even a little smile forms on her face. "If it ain't Daddy War-bucks coming back to his old stomping ground. I thought you done moved on up to the East Side to that deluxe apartment in the sky," joked Miss Bernice.

"Nice to see you too Miss Bernice," I said. "You've been getting the rent checks right?"

"Oh yeah, honey. Miss Bernice is real happy to have rent paid on time for a change. I've even taken you off my shit list." Several bar patrons laugh at me as I head upstairs. I notice a few changes have been made to the old place. "I like what you've done to the place Miss Bernice," I said.

"You do?" she asked while looking around.

"That's right. Too bad you still have the same old tired ass patrons." Bernice shakes her head as I walk upstairs to the office to wait on Michelle and Ken. As I walk inside the place almost seem foreign to me. Everything is as I left it. Daddy's framed photo is still on my desk. I look over at the Fern and amazingly it's still alive. I walk over and feel the soil to find out that it's moist. Miss Bernice is a softy after all.

A creaking noise on the floor causes me to spin around quickly with my gun pulled—James Bond style. My first day back and I get a visit from a ghost killer. "You won't need that," the man said. "Hiroshi I presume?"

"You remember me. That's good." His henchman is standing with him.

"I always make it a point to get to know the man that has me on the top of his hit list," I said. "Keep your hands where I can see'em." Hiroshi opens up his jacket to show he's not carrying. "What about your friend here?"

"This is Hadeo. He's my protection—just like you're protecting Ken Yamada. He is carrying," Hiroshi said.

"What can I do for you Mr. Ito? My time is valuable." I start to sweat inside, knowing that Michelle and Ken are due any moment. "Can I smoke?" Hiroshi asked. I keep one eye on Hadeo because he has tricky eyes. They can't be trusted. "Having a smoke with me implies that we're cool with one another—and we ain't cool."

"Then I'll get straight to the point. I could use a man like you in my organization. You give up Ken Yamada and join me. I'll make you a wealthy man," Hiroshi said.

"You see that sign on the door—it says Sam Phillips Investigations. That means I work for myself. I like working for myself because I hate taking orders Mr. Ito. I always have. Besides—I give up Ken Yamada to you and they find me with a bullet in the back, or my head chopped off Samurai style. That is the way you boys like to do it right?"

"You're making a big mistake Sam," Hiroshi said.

"My last girlfriend told me that exact same thing." Hiroshi calmly heads for the door with Hadeo leading the way. "This game is not over Sam Phillips!" As he walks out the door, I pick up the phone and quickly call downstairs to Miss Bernice.

"Miss Bernice—those guys that came up here are killers! They're coming down! They're looking for Michelle and Ken Yamada! Don't let them walk through that door or they're dead!"

Chapter 60

After dodging a bullet, the L.A. traffic must have slowed Michelle and Armstrong down. They arrive finally, looking drained—a sure sign of traffic fatigue. "It's the fucking 101 Freeway man!" Armstrong snaps. Michelle and Ken follow in behind. Michelle laughs at the big guy's annoyance. "It wasn't that bad. Try standing on a crowded train in Tokyo," she smirks. I quickly close the door behind them after taking a long look down the hall. My heart must have stopped several times worrying that Michelle and Ken would get caught in a cross-fire. Miss Bernice, I wasn't worried so much—the bullets would just bounce right off.

"Sam—you look like you just seen a ghost," Michelle said.

"It's funny you say that," I said. "Hiroshi just left ten minutes before you arrived, baby." Armstrong starts to pull his weapon. "Keep it clean big fella'. They're long gone." Armstrong looks around the crappy office with a curious look on his face. "I don't see bullet holes anywhere," he said. "They had the drop on me for a second or two too.

I guess they figure if they'd have killed me then finding Ken would be harder to do. He offered me a job in his organization—a high paying gig too," I joked.

"Let me guess. You'd have to give up the little guy here," Armstrong points out.

"What did you say Sam?" Ken asked. I patted Ken on the shoulder to reassure him.

"Don't worry Ken. I'm not that easily bought. He'd have to have thrown in a bucket of KFC also you dig." Ken laughs, but then looks over at Michelle.

"Sam, do you mind if I speak to my sister alone please?"

"Sure kid. Let's go 'Strong. Armstrong and I walk in the main office leaving Michelle and Ken behind.

240

Ken is pretty animated, arguing with Michelle as we stand in the doorway looking.

"Hey, man—they're going at it pretty heavy in there," Armstrong said.

"Whatever it is, it can't be good for us."

Hiroshi is a man on a mission. He's lost not only some of his best men, but he's lost his stranglehold on the power he held in Little Tokyo. Merchants no longer fear him. His businesses have been shut down, and his woman is dead. Instead of cutting and running back to Japan with his tail between his legs, Hiroshi has decided to replenish the ranks. Hiroshi and Hideo are at the airport terminal, waiting on the arrival of new recruits. As the men come inside the terminal from the International Flights, they greet Hiroshi and Hideo.

There's one man Hiroshi is waiting for in particular. His name is Mikio Suzuki—his main assassin, responsible for most of the murders of rival bosses of the Yakuza Clans.

Mikio arrives in the terminal, and one of the last to de-board the plane. Mikio's name means "Tree Trunk Man", which fits him to a T. He looks like a cross between a Sumo Wrestler and "Odd Job" from James Bond's Goldfinger. The Rebels are dressed like musicians in casual wear unlike the previous Rebels—to fool local law enforcement. Hiroshi is happy to see his old friend Mikio, and he greets him like a long lost brother.

"We have work to do," Hiroshi said in Japanese.

Chapter 61

I received a call from Miss Bernice telling me about a stuck up White girl in the bar waiting on me. She fits the description of one person, and that is Sidney Tolliver. Miss Bernice has had her feel of Sidney, and she warned me that she was about to throw the little "Baby Doll" out on her ass. When I arrive, I find Sidney being harassed by two guys on the bad side of any track. They were loud, and they didn't care who knew it.

Sidney, of course is, loving the attention. "Sam!" she said out loud. Sidney had a few drinks—somehow convincing Miss Bernice that she's twenty-one.

"C'mon Sidney—let's go upstairs."

"She ain't going nowhere, unless it's with us," one of the men said, grabbing my wrist.

"Let's all go upstairs!" Sidney said, tipsy. The other guy, who stands just north of Armstrong's height, gives me a shove up against the bar counter. I look down at my suit and notice a stain on the coat. "You just put a stain on my new suit, man," I said.

"Yeah—well what are you gonna' do about—" The next moment the big goon is on his knees from my kick to his balls, which he's picking up off the floor. "I forgot to tell you—I play dirty—always have." The other guy makes one move towards me, and I leveled him with a punch to the nose. "Didn't you just hear what I just said sucka'?!" I asked.

"I was just reaching to help Ernie up!" the man said, holding his nose. "You broke my nose!"

"Sorry about that." I grab Sidney and take her up to the office.

I get Sidney to the office as she plumps down on a chair in a un-lady like position all the while giggling like a schoolgirl. "You know, those big guys down there had big plans for you tonight—what the hell were you thinking?!" I asked firmly.

She struggles up from the chair and stumbles over to me. I've seen this picture before. Rich kid with everything handed to them in life, but can't handle the day to day challenges life can bring. Sidney has this struggle in spades.

"I wanted to come and find you as a Private Eye would," she stammers.

"Maybe I need to put you on the payroll," I answered back.

"You...couldn't afford me!" she said giggling. I throw my hat on the coat rack and take off my jacket, knowing Sidney was going to be a handful.

"That's the first sobering thing you've said to me baby." I check for messages even though I still haven't let Connie come back to the office yet. It's a force of habit I guess.

"What are you doing here Sidney?" Sidney looks around the room looking for something that I'm pretty sure I know what it is. "What do you have around here to drink?"

"Bingo!" I said to myself. "You've had enough little lady. I'm calling you a cab," I said, reaching for the phone. She quickly grabs my hand—stopping me from placing the call. "Wait! Please hear me out Sam," she said. The desperation in her voice is sending me vibes that spells trouble with a capital T. She takes her hand off of mines and sits back down finally, trying to gather her thoughts.

"I think my mother killed my father," she said somberly. Sidney just got my attention like a mobster whacking a snitch across the kneecap with a Louisville Slugger. It came out of left field alright, leaving me speechless for a moment. "Why would your mother hire a Private Dick knowing that I might stumble across a story like this?" I asked.

"I told back at the house—she wants to rejuvenate her acting career—so she hires a Private Detective to go around town asking questions to all the right people stirring interest in her again. She never gave it a second thought about me figuring out what she's doing. She gave me all the money and freedom I wanted to keep me quiet."

"But now you have a conscience?" I asked with sarcasm.

"You think you know me but you don't! Poor little rich girl you're probably thinking. Well, I loved my father, and I know he was murdered!"

"Your mother is my client baby. I just can't go and accuse her of murder."

"So it's about the money with you?" she asked, wiping tears away.

"You damn right!" I said, taking a hard stand. You never get involved is the credo we have in this business. Sidney reaches in her purse—fumbling for something in mind. "Okay fine! Then I'll make it worth your while!" she said. Sidney pulls out stack of crisp one hundred dollar bills and plants it on my desk. Here's a thousand dollars! There's plenty more where that came from! I want you to investigate my mother!"

"It's a conflict of interest baby. I can't go down that road. Put away your money. I'll have a friend at the precinct look into it for me. If he finds your story has some legs to it, I'll have him call you. That's all I can do for you." Sidney puts away her money, which I have a hard time letting get away. I must be going soft. Sidney plants a wet one across my lips, and it felt good I admit. "Thank you Sam," she said.

"Get outta' here before I change my mind."

Chapter 62

I make my way over to my mother's house where she's sitting for me with Saivon. The kid has taken to her, and my mother has finally come around to him. As my mother opens the door, Saivon
 greets me with a big hug. "How is my son?"
"I'm good Daddy! Granny showed me how to cook today!" he said, excited. His face is filled with white flour. "I see. Granny didn't work you too hard did she?" I asked.

"No. I like it a lot." I look at mom who's carrying the biggest smile on her face.

"We had a good ol' time," she said. "Someday, my grandson is going to join the family business, aren't you Saivon?" Momma asked.

"Yes ma'am." Momma reaches down and brushes a little powder off his face.

"Saivon you go and wash your face now so you can go home okay?" Granny said.

"Okay Granny!" Saivon rushes off to the bathroom giving my mother a chance to grill me about something because she has that look on her face like she's desperate to tell me something. "He is such a little angel son," she said.

"I hear a "but" coming," I said.

"There's no but. He's opened up about his mom, son. Have you tried looking for her?" I believe my mom was a victim of an invasion of the body snatchers. She seems to actually care now, unlike before when she gave me shit over getting a Vietnamese girl knocked up. I give her a hug and a kiss that surprises her. "What was that for?"

"I'm just glad you're here for me—that's all," I said. "I haven't looked for Mai yet. Where would I begin?" I asked.

"You're the Investigator son. You figure it out. I know one thing—you need to get on a plane and go over there and do what you do best," Mom said.

"It's not that easy Momma. There's someone else involved in all this," I said. My mother wasn't trying to hear that excuse from me. She fakes like she's reaching for the frying pan to knock me upside the head. "Boy! If there's a chance that Saivon's mother is still out there somewhere, then you move Heaven and Earth to find her! I didn't raise you any other way! You ain't too old that I can't go upside your head!" I laugh because my mother is so much shorter than me. When I was a kid and looking up at her, she made me wet my pants when she threatened me. "I promise Momma. Soon as I break from these two cases, I'm on the first flight to Vietnam."

After escaping my mother's wrath, I bring along Saivon on a trip to visit the grave of my father—Sam Phillips Sr. I hold my son's hand as we walk through all the graves of military veterans. My father was World War 2 and Korea and was awarded the Silver Star, but he never talked about his experience with war. Saivon lays down fresh flowers to the grave. "Is that where my grandfather is buried?" he asked.

"Yes son. He's there. But only his body is there. His spirit is looking down on us from Heaven."

"Is Heaven a good place?"

"It's a great place son." After a brief moment of silence, Saivon broke that silence like any kid his age would. "I'm hungry," he said.

Part Five   Return of the Rebel

Chapter 63

A dark cloud comes over Little Tokyo, as Hiroshi makes his return known. He enters the restaurant of Akio Fukoshima, who immediately starts to suck up to Hiroshi as soon as he makes contact with him. He bows continuously as he backs up toward the kitchen. Akio is at least thirty years older than Hiroshi, but he is made to gravel like a lap dog.

"Mister Hiroshi—I'm happy to see you again!" he said, squirming. Hiroshi looks around as if he owns the place, showing extreme arrogance and indifference to Akio.

"I heard your restaurant has made huge profits after I left Mr. Fukoshima," Hiroshi said. The chefs and the Sushi makers continue their duties knowing that seeing the gangster Hiroshi is business as usual.

"We've done okay sir, nothing to brag about."

"Are you calling me a liar?" Hiroshi asked. Akio takes a look at Mikio—a menacing individual and begins to choose what he says very carefully. "Oh no, sir, what I'm saying is we've had great weeks and some not so great weeks," Akio said in fear for his life.

Hiroshi picks up a just prepared sushi roll and eats it. "You will pay me for protection money that I didn't collect including what you owe me today," Hiroshi said calmly. "Mikio will make sure you give the right amount." Word gets around the community like a bad virus as Hiroshi goes to each business spreading his message like the pied piper he is. He's back, and this time it's for good.

I answer a call from the gang at the precinct about joining them at a police bar across from MacArthur Park off Wilshire and Alvarado. It's the safest business in the area because every low life knows a detective's cruiser when they see it. I get there after 6pm—just when the ladies of the evening are getting ready to go out on the stroll.

Everybody's got to get their hustle on, and in the community of Westlake, it's a 24 hour hustle.

The precinct is giving a toast to Joey and Tommy, so I knew I had to be here for them. I arrive inside, and you can tell that police know how to let loose some stress because they have all the elements to make a great party—booze, music, and hot chicks. "Sam! Over here, man!" Thompson shouts, waving me over. At the table with Thompson are Ozawa, Washington, and Captain Pierpont. The detectives are wearing t-shirts with a picture of Tommy and Joey on them. "What's up Detectives?" I asked.

"Sam!" everyone said. Ozawa hands me a t-shirt.

"There are hors d'oeuvres and stuff over there," Ozawa said. "Thanks for coming."

"I wouldn't be any other place Detective." I look across over at Pierpont, who raises his glass to me. "Phillips!" he snaps. "Joey always told me how you saved his life over in Vietnam! He'd tell me how you kept him from going insane by talking to him while you were in your foxholes or the bunkers at night.

He was the reason I allowed you in the precinct to see him."

"And all this time I thought it was my sweet disposition Captain," I joked. Everyone laughs. "Joey used to boast to the whole department how he and Tommy were Batman and Robin, and the rest of us were Snow White and the Seven Dwarfs," Ozawa said, laughing.

"Was I Snow White?" she asked.

"No—Washington is," Thompson joked. Hawkins and Rico Santiago from the task force have come over to join us. "Here's to Joey and Tommy, two great fucking cops!" Pierpont said, hoisting his glass.

After the dust clears, Hawkins reminds everyone that Hiroshi is back and is looking to take over Little Tokyo for good or take it down with him. "Hawkins is right," I said. "I had the privilege of running into Mister Ito in my office the other day. He had the drop on me for a split second too. He tried to recruit me to his organization."

"He's a resourceful little bastard isn't he," said Pierpont. Washington pulls out a marked bullet and spins it on the table. "I've got a bullet with his name on it."

Chapter 64

Crazy Willie has taken it upon himself to get hired at one of Hiroshi's businesses. Washing dishes at a nightclub and bar—Willie has worked for one week at the club and has made an impression on the other employees. Unfortunately for him, Hiroshi doesn't trust anyone lately, and has installed hidden cameras in certain areas where employees hang-out. Hiroshi and the club's manager—Stephen Tanaka is looking at the tapes of Willie talking to employees.

"He's been asking questions about you and the Black Rebels," Stephen said. Hiroshi has seen enough. He motions for his henchmen to bring Willie inside. "You see Stephen, technology will keep you ahead of your enemies all the time.

"The Black Rebels will be at the forefront of the latest technology of the future, which will keep us from being overtaken by ancient groups like the Yakuza." Stephen nods his head in agreement.

Willie is brought into Stephen's office with a choke hold from Mikio, whose carrying Willie by his neck.

"Hey man—I can walk wherever you want me to walk my brother! I'm a peaceful individual!" Willie said. Mikio lets go of Willie, who looks up at Mikio while rubbing his neck. Hiroshi laughs at the facial expressions Willie makes. "Oh you Black people are so funny!" Hiroshi said. "I'm glad I've amused you my man! Now who in the fuck are you?!"

Mikio holds up his big hand ready to strike, but Hiroshi waves him off. "I'm Hiroshi. I own this fine establishment," Hiroshi said. Willie looks over at Stephen for assistance that rolls on deaf ears. "Mr. Tanaka—help me out here sir." Stephen shrugs his shoulders.

"I heard you were a good worker Willie. I need good workers like you. I need people I can trust," Hiroshi said, slyly. Willie—being from the streets knows when a man says he needs people he can trust, he knows it means bend over and drop your pants.

"Can I trust you Willie?"

"Well…sure you can Mr. Ito," Willie said, nervous.

"How did you know my last name?" Hiroshi asked in suspicion. Willie looks around the room at all the Japanese men like he was a fish out of water. "Uhh…you told me my man," Willie answered back. "I told you my first name—Willie." Mikio slowly closes the blinds on the office windows. "Who sent you here Willie?" Hiroshi asked. Willie tries to back out but can't. It's like once you come in you can't get out, and Willie's stepped into the lion's den. "I must have heard someone say your name around here, man!" he pleaded.

"Are you a cop?" Hiroshi asked.

"No, I'm not a cop! I've been to prison!" Hiroshi pulls out his gun and places it against Willie's temple. "If you're not a cop, then you're working for the cops. It's because of people like you that made me lose everything including my girlfriend.

261

How do you Americans say… fool me once, shame on you—fool me twice, shame on me. You've made a grave mistake coming here, my brother."

Chapter 65

I got a call to come down to the Garment District in a back alley of a clothing store. When I get on the scene, Washington, and Ozawa are on the scene with the Crime Scene Unit that's just completed taping off the area. "What's up guys? I know I'm a great P.I., but isn't this a case for Homicide?" I asked.

"Homicide's giving us first crack at this case Sam," said Ozawa. I look up the alley and see Armstrong's Deuce and a Quarter coming down the street. "What's Armstrong doing here?" I asked. "I called him Sam," said Washington. The detectives are focused on a garbage dumpster as Armstrong makes his way through the crowd. "Who's in there?" I asked. "Brace yourself Sam," said Ozawa. As I look inside the dumpster, I immediately wanted to throw up. It's Crazy Willie, thrown in with the garbage with his throat cut from ear to ear. "They also cut out his tongue Sam," said Washington.

"It's a message that someone thought he was a snitch."
Armstrong is headed over, and I try unsuccessfully to
head him off.

"Armstrong—you don't want to see this brother!"

"You get outta' my way Sam!" Armstrong pushes me
out the way like a tornado moving through a trailer park.
He gets to the dumpster and lets out a big yell like only
he can. "WILLIE!!" As Armstrong grieves, Ozawa pulls
me to the side.

"My snitch told me that Willie took a job in Little
Tokyo working at a new club called The Red Sun,"
Ozawa said. "He said The Red Sun is owned by Hiroshi
Ito." Now I can put two and two together what happened.

"Willie tried to prove himself to me by getting a job
working for that asshole and probably got caught doing
what he's known for—running his mouth," I said.
Armstrong here's me tell what I think happened to Willie
and rushes at me with a look in his eyes I haven't seen
before. "This is your fault Sam!" Armstrong wraps his
hand around my throat and squeezes. "Willie tried to
make up for what he did to your father and now he's
dead! What the fuck am I gonna' tell my sister?!"

It takes several cops to pull Armstrong off me thank God, not a moment too soon. "I liked Willie too 'Strong!" I said, gasping. "But I didn't make him do what he did." I was right, but that didn't stop the big fella' from almost crushing my windpipe. It seems he almost blames himself for bringing in Willie

"Hiroshi don't know who he's fucking with," Armstrong growled. The M.E. arrives on the scene. He looks over Willie's body including his fingernails. He's helped out of the dumpster by Washington and Thompson. "Rigor mortis has set in gentlemen," the M.E. said. "I'd say this man has been dead at least five hours or more—putting his death at least between 10 and 12am last night." Willie's body is now pulled from the dumpster as a small crowd gathers. "I have to go and see my sister before this gets out," Armstrong said.

"Armstrong. I'm sorry man," I said. Armstrong can barely face me as he walks away.

"Yeah—I am too."

Chapter 66

A raid has went down on the Red Sun that night, but this
time Hiroshi had his men waiting for it. Meeting the
detectives inside the club is a paid high profile attorney
named Victor Lieberman. "This is an injunction
Detectives that prohibits you from harassing my client's
businesses. Thompson reads the paper and is not happy
with what he just read. He crumbles the paper up and
tosses it at Lieberman.

"How can you work for that cop killer?" he said. "I
sleep well at night Detective, how about you?"
Lieberman asked with sarcasm. Thompson makes a move
toward Lieberman but is held back by his fellow officers.

"You're sleaze, you got that?!" Stephen Tanaka is
laughing at the detectives while being handcuffed.

"Release my clients please," Lieberman said.

Seeing Willie like that really hit close to home. Not only have I lost Willie, but I may lose a good friend and partner in Armstrong. Seeing how hurt Armstrong was, I figured I better check in on Ken at the safe house. Carrying a six pack of Budweiser and my favorite—KFC chicken with me, I open the door, and Ken is waiting behind the door with a baseball bat. "I thought you were a burglar," he said.

"Yeah, a burglar with a key, and bringing beer kid," I told him.

"I'll take a beer!" We settle down to eat as I inform Ken of what happened today. When I tell Ken about what happened with me and Armstrong, he took it pretty hard. "But you two are partners!" he said with conviction. "Does this mean that Armstrong is not coming back Sam?" I toss another can of beer in the 13 gallon trash can that's now overflowing with beer cans and sandwich wraps. Ken, for no reason at all, starts to laugh. "What's so funny?" I asked. "I just realized I haven't had sex since I came to town," Ken said. I have to admit the kid has held out for a month before caving in.

That's longer than I've ever gone. "I can bring you a couple of magazines tomorrow and you can choke the snake until it falls off you dig?"

"That's not sex—I want a girl man!" he said. Ken goes into the bedroom and brings out a magazine—a Players Magazine; Dark Chocolate sista's in all their glory. "I want a fine Black girl!" he said, like a horny kid in puberty. "Who am I, your pimp, kid? Besides, I can't have anyone else in here—you know that." Ken runs his fingers over the pages as if the model was there. "I'm gonna' have to get rid of Hiroshi because your demands are starting to get ridiculous," I said.

"So—does that mean…"

"Alright Ken. I can get that done—but not on our home turf. We have to go to the visitor's park you dig?" Ken kisses the model on the magazine.

"I dig it!"

Chapter 67

I take Ken to a place over in Inglewood that has a five-star rating, I heard through the grapevine. There's no neon signs needed as this place features a lot of repeat business. We're greeted by the hostess named Lola, who's dressed in black lace that barely covers up her "assets".

"There's a ten dollar cover charge to go in, gentlemen," she said with a gap toothed smile.

"This is just for my little friend here sweetheart," I said.

"You look like the fuzz suga'. You're not trying to bust us are you?" Lola asked, with a charming smile. "Some of L.A.'s finest always showing up here threatening to shut us down just so they can get their boogie on."

"I wouldn't dream of taking advantage of anyone trying to make a buck these days baby." I hand Lola a twenty for her trouble.

She buzzes an extremely happy Ken in, leaving me behind with Lola, which with my 20/20 vision—ain't all that bad. "What can I do to make you more comfortable while you wait for your friend?" Lola asked, with a tempting look. "Baby, I wish you would have asked me that, six months ago." Twenty minutes was an eternity, as I get a smile and a wink by several different ladies with barely a stitch of clothing on. Ken comes out with his escort, who has her arm around him, and a smile as wide as the Grand Canyon. "Now you make sure you come back and ask for me again now suga'," his escort said. She kisses Ken on the mouth and squeezes his butt. Lola hands me a business card. "If you're ever in the need…you pick up the phone and call Lola."

"Let's go Casanova," I said. I figure I'd better leave before I change my mind. Ken is skipping like a kid who just had a trip to Disney World.

I decided to go back to Hollywood after dropping Ken off at the safe house to get a stiff drink at Miss Bernice's place. I'll even take some verbal abuse from Miss Bernice tonight—a man could use a good punch in the face to make him see things more clearly. The bar is empty except for a few regulars.

"Miss Bernice, give me a stiff one," I said, crashing down on a stool.

"What are you doing here Sam? Why aren't you at home taking care of your new family?" she asked with her sharp sarcasm digging at me like a knife. "Oh, Miss Bernice...I can always count on you to kick a man when he's down. It's a quality I respect most in you." Miss Bernice laughs while pouring my drink. "How is your boy, anyhow?" she asked.

"I want to say he's a chip off the ol' block, but he's a lot smarter than I was at his age." I down the first shot glass and I instruct Miss Bernice to keep'em coming. "I heard about Crazy Willie Sam. He was one of a kind, and that's for sure," Miss Bernice said. "You know Sam, Willie told me something once that I didn't think about much until today. He told me that he blew it with your father and that he wished he could have followed in your father's footsteps. I guess he was trying to prove something for you." Like I said—Miss Bernice knew how to kick a man when he's down. The guilt from hearing that makes me sick to my stomach that I didn't reach out more to Willie.

"You're right Miss Bernice. Willie was trying to prove something to me, but I guess I wasn't listening." I finished off the last glass of Bourbon and had to be helped upstairs to my office by my landlord to sleep it off.

Chapter 68

After waking up in my clothes from the night before, I knew I blew it with seeing my son off to school. My pounding headache gave me some serious thought about what Miss Bernice had to say about family. I made a pit stop first before returning to Connie's place. It at least looks like it's going to be a beautiful day, as fall has kicked in as I make my way home. Home—it sounds like a cheesy Kodak moment—a son, a good woman to come home to.

   I put my key in the door, but Connie beat me to it. She must have been waiting at the door patiently like a Black Widow Spider, waiting for its male mate to bring lunch—himself. "Where were you Sam, your son was asking about you all morning?!" Connie said with her nostrils flaring like they were breathing fire. "I went to the office last night, and I must have fallen asleep," I said. It was a good excuse given, as it seems to stop Connie in her tracks.

"You could have called me like you, usually, do—I was worried sick." I give her a kiss on the cheek and a hug which suddenly gave her more ammunition. Any woman with more ammunition against you is like the equivalence of African Soldier Ants wiping out every living thing in its path.

"Looks like you've been drinking. I can smell it on your clothes and your breath. You mind telling me where you really were?" Connie asked.

"I had to go to the safe house. Armstrong went AWOL baby. I had drinks with Ken, and we talked all night." Connie rubs my face with her hand, as she believes me now. She knows I can't lie about a case because she can easily check the story. This case is starting to take its toll on all of us Sam. When is it going to end?" she asked.

"It's going to end when it ends, baby," I said. "Do you want to go back to getting one client a week, or going through old files? Right now we have people calling everyday for our services—enough so that we may have to take on another investigator.

And our recent success has allowed me to do this…" I reach in my pocket and pull out a diamond ring. The reaction on Connie's face says to me that I must have made a good decision for once. I bend on one knee like I know Billie Dee Williams would. "Connie, would you marry me?" I asked. Connie has a shocked look on her face—in a good way, but that's not helping my bended knee. "Sam…you haven't once told me you loved me," Connie said.

"I know—that's why I'm giving you this ring. I love you Connie. Connie holds the ring in her hand while thinking it over. Sam, I can't marry you now. I want you to marry me when I can see the love you have for me in your eyes," she said.

Why do women over think things so much? This begging crap is not what the early man had in mind. He would hit a woman over the head with his club, and she would know she was his woman. "Connie, you read too many romance novels," I said. "We're two adults who have worked together, and came together."

"Came together?! Is that what you think we've done?" Now this feels like a marriage. Everything a man does is wrong in a woman's mind. "I'm sorry—you're right baby. I should have waited until the time was right. Can you forgive me?" That was music to Connie's ears as she lays a wet one on my lips. I'm getting better at this relationship thing.

Chapter 69

An anonymous tip has brought the task force into Little Tokyo. Parked quietly on the street in broad daylight, Hawkins and his crew, including Rico, Ozawa, and Thompson packed readily to go to war if there's any resistance. It's 10:00am and Hiroshi was spotted going into a massage parlor. Ozawa is on the street as a lookout and dressed like a typical citizen of the community. There was a rain shower an hour ago that can still be smelled throughout the neighborhood. Festival signs are posted throughout the streets for the upcoming fall events.

"Okay boys and girls, we want this by the book," Hawkins instructed. "This is one Harry Houdini we're dealing with here. If he gives you any resistance –put him down like the dog he is." A "copy that" is given by the team. It's been over an hour and no signal yet from Ozawa. "Why don't we just bust in and grab him sir?" Rico asked.

"Because I'm sure he has people in there to signal him if there's a raid. It could get messy," Hawkins said. "When he comes out front, we'll have him trapped like John Dillinger." A man matching Hiroshi's description comes out of the building with one bodyguard—Hadeo, wearing dark glasses and a heavy fall jacket. Ozawa, sitting on a bench acting as if she's having a lunch break, gives the signal. "It's him," she said. Suddenly, men and women jump out of nowhere and surround Hiroshi and Hadeo. Hadeo opens his jacket displaying two handguns in his waistband.

"Throw down your weapons or say goodbye motherfucker!" Rico shouts. Hadeo freezes in his tracks as the task force rushes in. Hawkins walks in knowing he's got his man.

"Hiroshi Ito, you're under arrest for the murder of Detective's Tommy Sato, and Joey Sorvino," he said.

Hiroshi laughs at the attention. People are gathering around the street to watch in amazement as Hiroshi is being read his rights and handcuffed. "You've got nothing on me Officer. I only killed someone breaking into my home and killing my girlfriend. It was self-defense," he said laughing.

A task force officer knocks Hadeo's shades off as he's being led away.

"My lawyer will have me out before dinner," Hiroshi boasts. As Hiroshi's is being led away, Hawkins and Rico discuss the way it should have gone down. "I'm afraid he may be right Rico," Hawkins said. "I was so hoping he would resist sir," Rico said. "You give me the word and I'll make sure we take a detour on the way to the precinct." Hawkins shrugs his shoulders knowing he missed a golden opportunity. "In a perfect world Rico I will—in a perfect world."

Hiroshi and Hadeo are brought into the precinct and walk through a gauntlet of detectives and police officers who would like nothing but to rip their heads off. "Give'em room boys," O'Halloran said. "We don't want them to trip and fall. They could break their freakin' neck." A sea of blue surrounds the gangsters like being swallowed up by a Blue Whale. The two men are escorted to processing for fingerprinting and booking. News travels fast, as the Press gets wind of the arrests, and they swarm on the precinct like a plague of locusts. The Press is firing questions at Captain Pierpont in rapid succession as the police hold them back.

"Yes we have made an arrest but we have just begun in the process. You all know how this works. Please let us do our jobs!" Pierpont said.

Chapter 70

I received a call from the Tolliver home to come out there immediately. The last time I talked to Sidney, things were getting ugly at home. She believed her mother had something to do with her father's disappearance. Jealousy and envy between a mother and daughter is nothing new, but somehow I get the impression Sidney's drinking was masking an even darker secret.

I still haven't heard from Armstrong yet, so I asked Detective Ozawa to sit in for me with Ken. Being that she's Japanese, Maria can relate to Ken's plight. Maria had it rough. Coming from Japan as a child, she had it hard growing up in Downey, California.

When Maria joined the police force, she had faced racial and sexual discrimination at the precinct before she was finally accepted. As I drive onto the Tolliver's block, I notice lights of police and emergency vehicles. And they're parked in the Tolliver driveway. I park on the street, and as I walk up the driveway, I'm met by Harold, who is very upset.

"What's happened Harold?" I asked.

"There was a terrible accident sir!" Harold said, in shock. Lauren Tolliver is wheeled out of the house on a stretcher— fortunately not covered up, with paramedics working on her. I try to work my way over to her, but am stopped by police. "No one gets through buddy," the officer said.

"It's okay Officer, I'm a relative," I fired back. The poor cop didn't know how to handle that answer it came out so fast and confidant. I walk by him to grab Lauren's outstretched hand. "What's happened Mrs. Tolliver?" I asked. Lauren looks at the media forming outside the mansion. "How do I look Sam?!" she asked.

"You're a knock out Lauren."

"We have to go sir," the paramedic said in a hurry. Lauren has a smile on her face, as she waves to her audience. Sidney is brought out in handcuffs with an expensive scarf wrapped around them. That's how the Beverly Hills Police treat one of their own. Sidney stops when the police bring her toward me on her way to the car. A determined reporter gets through so he could get the first response from the young socialite. "Sidney—did you shoot your mother?!" he shouted. I shove the bum to the ground on his ass, prompting him to drop his equipment. "Hey—did you see that officer?!" the reporter asked.

"Can't say that I did," the officer said, smiling. The officers let me take Sidney to the car. "I didn't mean to do it Sam."

"I know kid. It was one of those days," I said. The cameras begin to click away at the blonde beauty. "What's going to happen to me now?" she asked soberly.

"Don't worry about it Sidney—it's Beverly Hills. Just be yourself—you'll have them eating right out of your hands."

Sidney was right all along. Lauren was seeking the publicity she craved, and she got it. And me—I was the sucker that she was looking for, and I danced to her tune like a Soul Train regular. At least the pay was good—while it lasted.

Chapter 71

I was told about the arrest of Hiroshi Ito—a man whose popularity has quickly turned Capone type status. He's placed in the interrogation room once used by the detectives he's accused of killing. I was asked to come down and sit in on the interrogation by Captain Pierpont, who has decided with Detective's Washington and Thompson to do the honors.

The detectives gang up on Hiroshi like a tag team bent on making the gangster slip up and make a mistake. "You killed Detective Sorvino because he accidently killed your girlfriend, right?!" Thompson asked forcefully. "I believe in this country I have a right to make a phone call," Hiroshi stated. "I have a moral right to have my foot up your ass too!" Washington said, grabbing at Hiroshi as Thompson holds him back.

Thompson looks out at the two-way mirror where Pierpont and I are watching. "We know about your feud with the Yakuza," Thompson continued. "You murdered your rivals to take over their territory—you actually did the community a favor with that one, but you had to have it all like Caesar."

"Yeah, and just like Caesar my man—you're going down hard. It's just a matter of how hard," Washington said. Hiroshi laughs and reaches for another cigarette across the table with his handcuffs still intact. "You two cops are funny like Dean Martin and Jerry Lewis. I don't know which of you the "straight man" is. You have no evidence of me doing anything wrong.

I killed in self-defense. Who will answer for the killing of my girlfriend? Two of the men who were there that day are now dead, but I didn't kill the other one." If Hiroshi were on the other side of the law, he'd make one hell of a lawyer the way he's handling the detectives. "We have two witnesses that saw you in the hospital when you killed Detective Sato, my man," said Thompson, getting in Hiroshi's face. Hiroshi slowly backs away from Thompson and stares out at the two-way mirror.

"Anybody can buy witnesses. I have plenty of witnesses also.

I have very loyal witnesses that will say I wasn't in that hospital at all Detectives. You know what they say—all Asians look alike." He bursts out laughing—taunting the detectives, prompting them to walk out the room in disgust. The two witnesses are brought in the waiting area while, at the same time, Hiroshi's attorney shows up. His name is Larry Rothschild, a high priced sleaze-ball attorney who loves high profile cases that would give him a chance to show his pretty face in front of the camera. He's represented athletes in trouble for drug arrests and rape and celebrities of all shapes and sizes who can't keep their nose clean.

He looks inside the interrogation room and blows a gasket. "Why is my client being interrogated without his attorney present Captain?!" he asked.

"Larry, why is it every time there's a sleazy suspect in my station, here you come just wiped off the bottom of someone's shoe?"

"Because I'm the best Captain, even Hollywood knows it. That's why I'm the technical advisor on several shows,"

Larry gushed, dousing his mouth with breath spray. Larry enters the room at the disdain of Pierpont, O'Halloran, and me. "I passed a gallstone last week—I named it Rothschild," O'Halloran stated with a straight face. "Did you step on it with your shoe?" Pierpont asked. Inside the room, Rothschild proved why he's the best, as he has Hiroshi's full respect. "Look at him in there," Thompson said. "He's dancing around Ito like a fuckin' peacock." Ramona struts in front of all the testosterone-laden men with a painted on skirt. "Captain—they're ready for you," she said. She looks at me as if to say; "Look at all this you're missing mutha' fucka'!" She breaks up tension in the hall for a moment as only she can, as we all clear our throat and get back to the business at hand.

"Detective Thompson—would you be so kind as to ask the suspect in there if he wouldn't mind standing in a lineup please," Pierpont said. Rothschild, Hiroshi's lawyer, convinces him to stand in the lineup while two nurses who were on staff that night, try to pick him out. All the men are placed in a lineup dressed alike which makes the detective's nervous. "Hell…there's no way I can even pick him out," said Thompson.

"It'll be a miracle if they choose our guy."

It's an impossible task for the witnesses to be sure, and Hiroshi knows it. That same smirk on his face is the one he gave me in my office when he offered me a job after trying so hard to kill me. "Take your time ladies," Pierpont said nervously. He sees Hiroshi slipping through his fingers, and his ass chewed out by the police chief if things go south.

"I'm sorry—I'm just not sure," one nurse said.

"Look again!" Pierpont suggested. This maneuver doesn't sit well with Rothschild.

"The lady said she wasn't sure Captain. That is doubt in my book." The other nurse shakes her head. "I'd hate to send the wrong man to prison," she pointed out. Rothschild smiles like a snake with a full belly. "You'll release my client as soon as possible Captain." The captain, upset over the witness's lack of confidence, still has one card up his sleeve.

"I think we'll keep him until he faces the judge in the morning for the killing of Detective Sorvino. And he tried to kill Sam here who was in that room." I nod my head in agreement with the captain. Even if it wasn't true I probably would have done it anyhow. The guy just rubs me the wrong way. "Okay Captain—we'll play it your way.

You're just prolonging the inevitable. My client was returning from a business meeting when you stormed his home and killed his precious girlfriend. I'll have the jury weeping in their seats when I'm done." Rothschild leaves to see to Hiroshi, leaving Pierpont steaming.

"I really hate that guy."

Chapter 72

Hiroshi did get to see the judge the next morning. Against the wishes of the prosecution, the judge granted Hiroshi bail, set at $200,000 dollars, which Hiroshi happily paid his twenty percent. It's another setback for everyone involved who wants to see justice in the deaths of my two friends. One of the people pissed off is Detective Ozawa, who I just relieved from watching Ken.   She's a little tired, but she's used to it from doing "stakeouts" she told me. "I can't fuckin' believe they've let that killer out on the streets again!" she barked. She throws a soda can across the room in anger. I laugh because she didn't quite get the effect she wanted.

"Is that all you got Ozawa?" Embarrassed, she laughs as well along with Ken. "I guess you can do better." I crumble up a can and give it a Bob Gibson wind up and pitch—sailing the can across the room and smashing up against the wall.

"Not bad Sam," she said.

"I played the game baby." Instead of driving home, Maria stayed around to shoot the breeze with us for a while. She laid some heavy shit on me during the night, including her desire to leave the force. "You wanna' do what?!" I asked, surprised.

"I'm sick of all the bullshit man. You see it Sam. We arrest the bad guys, but that's not enough man."

"Yeah, but at least the big gangsters get arrested here in the states," Ken said. "In Japan, the bosses never see a day in jail." We go back and forth about the differences in the two country's justice system of fighting back crime until Ozawa hits me over the head with a whammy. "I'd like to come and work with you as a Private Detective," she said.

It's a bold statement she laid on me, and I'm still sober. Whoever heard of a female Private Eye? It ain't kosher. "You wanna' be a Private Dick, Ozawa? Now why would you want to put yourself through all the embarrassment that comes with this job?" I asked. "Its long hours with little pay and no benefits—"

"You mean like being a cop?"

"Well...okay you got me there. I just don't know if the public's ready for a female Private Investigator."

"Are you ready for it Sam?" I guess the little lady's got a point. If the public finally accepted a Black man doing this job, I don't see why it won't accept a woman. "Well, you are licensed to carry a weapon already. That's cool in your favor," I said.

"I have a lot of unsolved cases that we can tackle," she suggested. Ozawa is encouraged at the thought of teaming up. She's practically bouncing off the wall with excitement. "Before I offer you the position you have to understand that you'd be behind Armstrong in seniority. He's been there for me from the start," I said.

"How do you know if he's coming back?"

"If I had a farm to bet—I'd bet it that Armstrong is coming back. As long as you know that, then I love to have you. Until you get your license and retire from the force, you can moonlight for now. Great—now Captain Pierpont is going to start hating me all again for taking one of his detectives away. Ain't that a Bitch?!"

Chapter 73

The nightmares continue to haunt me as I make a stop at the office to do some paperwork on the Tolliver case. Some say the dreams I have could stay with me for the rest of my life. How in the hell does anyone know. The Tolliver Case: a study of the privileged few. I learned a lot with that case. It taught me the old saying; if it seems too good to be true, it usually is. I reach across my desk to pick up my father's picture, standing next to his new car.

He was very happy that day. I shipped off to war three months later. Suddenly I hear footsteps slowly coming down the hall. I reach for my weapon as I look at the shadow of footsteps underneath the door. I turn off the lamp and cock my trusty .45. A key turns the doorknob letting in a big and dark silhouette. "You take one more step, and it may be your last," I said. "It's me—Armstrong!" The big fella' steps in like a long lost pup that found its way home.

"I was just about to open up a new bottle of Remy Martin. Get a glass," I said. The big guy tosses his hat on the coat rack and smiles as I turn the lamp back on.

"I can use a stiff one," he tells me.

We sit and drink for about ten minutes before saying a word, not because of the awkwardness but because we've been so comfortable around each other. We didn't have to say much—just like an old marriage. I reach in the desk drawer and pull out an envelope and hand it to Armstrong. "Your license finally came in today.

You are now an official Private Investigator," I said. "You've come a long way my friend. We are still friends aren't we?" Armstrong picks up the envelope and smiles.

"You damn right brother!" We take turns drinking each other under the table and not mentioning the rift we had in the first place. "So who helped you watch Ken while I was gone?" Armstrong asked. "Maria Ozawa. I learned a lot about her. She also wants to join us as an Investigator. Don't worry, I told her she'd be third in line." Armstrong takes a moment and then bursts out laughing. "Let me get this right. We have two brotha's and Tokyo Rose Investigations! We can make our own Kung Fu movie!" Armstrong cracked.

We joked around and talked shop until I realized I have a woman and child to get home to. "I'll close up boss—your family needs you more than I do," Armstrong said. I agreed with Armstrong—especially after Connie read me the riot act last time. I take off like I stole something, leaving the big man to close shop. Armstrong finally leaves the office, not after first having a couple more drinks. He staggers down to his car parked on Vine Street just across from Capitol Records. He tries to get in the car but drops the keys on the ground. "Man, I am too drunk to drive," he said out loud. A motorcycle gang pulls around the corner onto Vine—roaring in the quiet night.

They pull up alongside Armstrong and take off their helmets revealing themselves. It's Mikio—the assassin of Hiroshi, with a small group of killers. "You guys…look like a bunch of cartoon characters." Mikio smiles as he gets off his bike. "Are you the man who terrorized Little Tokyo gangsters?" Mikio asked. "I am disappointed. Instead of meeting a fellow warrior you turn out to be a drunk."

"I'll show you drunk. Can a drunk-ass man do this, jive turkey'?" Armstrong lifts the one side of his Buick Electra 225 up in the air to pick up his keys. Mikio's men are shocked at Armstrong's strength.

Mikio waves his hand at his men who climb off their bikes in unison. Dressed in colorful attire, they stand out, even in Hollywood. "Kill him," Mikio commands.

The men race toward Armstrong and surround him in a circle like a pack of wolves. They come at Armstrong in waves, but are turned back by a force of nature greater than themselves—Armstrong is built for this shit. Many bones are being crushed by him, as the gangsters yell like wounded dogs.

"Ain't this fun?!" Armstrong shouts—covered in blood—most of it not from him. Not until the men started pulling out blades and swords were things starting to change.

Armstrong is sliced and diced like meat on a cutting board as he continues to fight. He's stabbed in the stomach—bringing him down to his knees.

"Are you still having fun—mother fucker?!" Mikio asked badly. Mikio slowly pulls out his sword to finish Armstrong off. "I'm going to make an example of you—warrior. Nobody messes with the Yokohama Black Rebels. You can lose your head if you do." Beaming lights flash in Mikio's face and sirens blast as Armstrong slumps to the ground. Mikio and his men jump on their bikes and roar off into the night leaving Armstrong in a pool of blood.

Chapter 74

I get a call from the Hollywood Division telling me to haul ass to the hospital. They told me that Armstrong is in critical condition from a brutal attack. They found his P.I. License on him that displayed my information as good as my dog tags. Armstrong wouldn't go down without a fight. If he's in critical condition, the other guys must be dead.

I made it to the Emergency wing and was quickly escorted out of Armstrong's room. "You can't come in sir!" a nurse barked. It looks like the whole hospital staff is in the room working on the big man. "He's losing more blood!" a doctor said. I come to the realization that I might lose my friend. I see a police officer and work my way through the throng of live bodies to get to him. "I'm Private Detective Sam Phillips. I got a call—"

"Oh yeah—that was me," the officer said. "I have never seen a man beat up like that before. It looks a train rolled through Vine Street, and he was tied to the tracks. There was a lot of blood on the street, but all of it wasn't his. Some of the suspects must need hospital care."

The doctor comes out with a face so unreadable he'd make a "killing" playing poker. "Give it to me straight Doc," I said. "If he makes it through the night he has a fifty, fifty chance of making it. We've stopped the bleeding, must he has massive trauma to his vital organs from multiple stab wounds. A normal man would already be in the morgue."

A code blue goes off for another patient. "Excuse me—I have to go!" Hearing that Armstrong has a fighting chance makes me want to find the culprits even more. And I know exactly whose door to knock on. "I can see you have that look in your eye, Mr. Phillips. This crime happened in Hollywood. Let us handle it."

"Officer—my badge says Private—Investigator. That means I have no jurisdiction. My partner got butchered outside his office. Look in my eyes and tell me what kind of look I have now." Hiroshi has drawn first blood on my turf now.

He's declared war on me—I know all about war, and I know just who to call. Armstrong is placed in Intensive Care with stitches and bandages covering his entire body. I stand next to his bed and realize how helpless he is. "I'm not going to let you end up like Tommy man, even if I have to stay by your bed every day."

"If you do that you're going to be one funky dude— soldier," a man said. I turn around to this familiar voice to see my old army buddy—Cleavon "Mongol" Monroe. Cleavon took a Genghis Khan approach to wiping out the enemy—he annihilated them. "Mongol—hey man!" We hug each other for the first time in three years. Cleavon's buzz cut is now a large afro, but other than that, he still looks the same. "What the hell are you doing here brotha'?!" I asked. "We heard about Joey from your secretary," he said. "When I called her, she told me where you were headed."

"Who is "we"?" I asked.

"I wouldn't come to a fellow Army brother empty handed man." Rushing into the room comes three other friends from my platoon. Glen "Casper" Zimmerman; he was anything but a friendly ghost. He was a quiet assassin. Buck Johnson was our weapons expert. And Gary "Hardcore" Danielson; everything that came out of his mouth was about the Military.

He talked about being a career soldier, and he'd knock you on your ass if you spoke ill of the Military in his presence. I have to admit it was a tearful reunion. Gary, still dressed in uniform, prayed for Armstrong and us as we stayed by his bedside the rest of the night.

Chapter 75

Armstrong survived the night, and the doctor said he has a good chance of full recovery. I brought the guys back to Connie's place where she was all too happy to cook breakfast for the former grunts. As we wait for breakfast, I pass around pictures of Saivon to the guys like the proud father I am. "He's a great looking kid," Gary said. Gary gets out his wallet to display that he has an Amerasian kid too. The other guys pull out pictures of their kids. It eerily turns into a male version of a Tupperware party or something. Connie is amused at the picture of us tough guys and smiles at me. "I do remember you and that little beauty of yours—what was her name…?" Buck asked. "Her name was Mai," I said. "No one knows, man. She dropped Saivon off during the fall of Saigon's last days. I'm not even sure she's alive."

"You have to find out brother," Casper said. The rest of the guys echo Casper's sentiments too. Connie puts on a brave face.

I give the heads up to cool it. Cleavon steps up and throws me a life line. "So…uh, you become a P.I. like your old man, you meet this fine sista', a cool pad—shit that's outta' sight Sam!"

"The job was a given my man. Connie was the icing on the cake. She's been my rock man."

"I heard that!" Cleavon said.

"Breakfast is ready boys." Connie only had to say it once, just like a mess hall, and no one had to come and force us to come and get it while it's hot. Over breakfast, we talk of some good times while in Country, skipping over the bad shit—we had enough of that, including discussing Agent Orange. Thank God I came after the operation stopped. "Constance told me about what happened to Joey, and that you could use a little help with this Japanese gang," Cleavon said. "I figured you wouldn't ask for my help, so I called the guys, and here we are."

I look over at Connie who's eating her food quietly, as a person who's thinking now for the both of us. Ramona sure as hell would not have done such a gesture. "I hope you're not mad I went behind your back," Connie said.

I reach under the table and grab Connie's hand and give it a squeeze.

"I wouldn't have had it any other way baby."

The guys go through Connie's food with the precision of a beaver going through wood. Not any evidence of leftovers on their plates. "Looks like you missed your calling Constance," Buck said. "That was the best homemade breakfast I've had in a long time."

"Why thank you Buck. My mother always taught me a way to a man's heart is through his stomach," Connie said. The guys look at my way and laugh.

"Well, you two should be ready to jump the broom then because his stomach is bloated like a beached whale!" Casper joked. I give Connie the checkbook to go shopping for office supplies just so that me and the guys can go over some plans. I wanted her to get out and get some fresh air. She hasn't had a break since this case started.

Chapter 76

I make fresh coffee for the guys after cleaning up the dishes and the kitchen. I get laughed at me being domesticated, but it's cool. "That's one foxy lady you have Sam," Cleavon said.

"Any sista' that can cook like that is cool in my book," Gary cuts in.

"Yeah, but when are you going to make an honest woman of her my brother?" Buck asked. "She's not a shack up sort of chick. This pad is cool too, but you need a house." Buck loads his coffee with six spoons of sugar and stirs it with his finger to suck the taste. I look around the crib and begin to get his point. "How can we help you Sam?" Cleavon asked. "Joey was a friend you dig?" I look at my watch and realize the day is moving on quickly.

"I don't want you guys getting in too deep. I can use some help with surveillance and security for my friend in the hospital—which reminds me I have to get over there." I get up from the table and am stopped by Gary's hand on my shoulder. "My kid sister has a big spread out in the valley. I can put these guys up for the time you need us."

"Don't you guys have lives to get back to?" I asked. Cleavon walks over and rests his hand on my shoulder too. "We'll give you fourteen days my brother. We'll exterminate this mother fucka' with extreme prejudice you dig?" Buck and Casper walk over to join in.

"Right on, man!" I said. We put our hands in together like we did in the service. We slap hands and pop our fingers in unison.

I make it back to the hospital to check in on Armstrong, who's still in Intensive Care, but there's a glimmer of hope as the big guy opens his eyes for the first time. I made arrangements with hospital security to have a decorated Veteran watch over Armstrong. Gary has agreed to watch over my partner; a man he doesn't even know because that's what Brother's in Arms do.

310

There were no witnesses to Armstrong's attackers, but I'd stake my reputation on betting it was Hiroshi's men. The nurse comes in to check up on him by caring for his bandages. "His eyes are open nurse," I said. "Yes—he's been responding in and out all morning. The doctors think the worst is over." I squeeze Armstrong's hand as I bend down to get closer for him to hear me. "You hear that 'Strong? The doctor's say you're getting better!" Armstrong closes his eyes again. It's a sign that Gary recognizes. "It's the drugs man. He's flying in the clouds like Superman." The nurse laughs at Gary's assessment while explaining the need for the drugs. "Your friend is a very strong man. But even Superman had Kryptonite that could kill him. Mr. Jones is lucky to be alive. He's probably reliving the assault in his mind," she said.

"I can relate to that," I said. Entering the room are two detectives from the Hollywood Police Department.

They're dressed in plain clothes, with a street edge which signals that they're from Narcotics or the Vice Squad.

They flash their badges and give their names; Detective's Brian Holt and James Pappas, a Serpico look alike. "What can we do for you Detective's?" I asked.

The two men take one look over at Armstrong—a dark man and make an assumption about what must have gone down. "Your friend—Mr. Armstrong wasn't involved in a drug transaction that went bad was he?" Pappas asked. Straight out of the blue he basically accused Armstrong of being a drug pusher.

"He works with me Detective. He was attacked outside our office."

"He just got out of prison." The detective fired back.

"Armstrong was the victim here man!" I growled back. Gary holds me back and tries to calm everyone down. "Detective, this man means a lot to Sam here."

"Stay out of this—baby killer!" Holt demanded. "That's right. I heard about what you guys were doing over there." Gary throws up his hands in a peaceful manner.

"Hey—you've got the authority here Detective. I'm just here to give support to my buddy here," Gary said. The nurse is disgusted and has had enough.

"I'm going to have to ask you all to leave. You're disturbing the patient!" she quietly barked. Holt and Pappas realize that Armstrong won't be going anywhere for a while in his condition.

They can afford to be patient—for now. "Something went down last night, and we want to know what," said Pappas. "Believe me; you don't want to be on our bad side."

Chapter 77

I left Gary with Armstrong while I go and take care of a situation that was brought to my attention by the guys. I called my buddy Stan Shapiro, a Real Estate friend who I did some work for on occasion. He was a good friend of my father's and a client. He asked me to drop by his office in Sherman Oaks to discuss things. Stan is a married father of three, but his wife suspects him of cheating on her with his young beautiful secretary with the killer body.

Stan is a veteran of the forgotten Korean War with a Purple Heart that he sometimes displays to his clients—hey, anything for a sale man. I walk inside the office as Stan is finishing up with a client. He waves at me while doing his sales pitch.

"How are you doing Sam?!" he asked, giving me a big hug.

"You know me Stan—one case at a time man," I answered back.

"Come on back, I have something to show you," Stan said, pulling me by the arm. We walk back to his desk that has a stack of fresh clients on it—unlike my desk. His wall is littered with awards and famous clients shaking hands or kisses from the famous women like Zsa Zsa Gabor, Raquel Welch and Elizabeth Taylor. Stan is the "man" in this town. Stan picks up a picture of my father and me when I was about fifteen years old. "Remember when that photo was taken?" he asked. The photo brings back fond memories for me.

"Yes I remember," I said with sentiment. "We had just moved out here less than a year."

"That was when my office was located in Mid-town—the good ol' days."

"Yeah—Sunset and Western, man. You had introduced my father to a law firm over there. He said it was the help that jump-started his career," I said. Stan holds onto the picture with a strong grip. I forget that this must have fond memories for him too. "Your father was a good man Sam—one of the best I ever met. I want you to have this picture."

"I can't take—"

"Take it," he insisted. Stan gets out a white handkerchief and wipes his face. Something is telling me that something else may be bothering Stan other than an old photo. "I have just the house for you and your girlfriend. Let's take a ride," he said. We take a drive over to Stan's old stomping grounds to Mid-town to a street lined with Palm Trees and plenty of Sunshine. We stop at a one story house with a connected garage with front and back yards to match. "This can't be the home you're referring to me is it? I can't afford this." Stan gives me a smile as we get out of the car and walk in the front gate. "This is the house I first thought of when you called. It needs a little work, but it's a steal at thirty thousand," he said. I almost swallowed my tongue at the price quote, but Stan doesn't flinch.

"Trust me. With my connections, you can get the financing you need to own this home." We go in the house and once we started looking around I was starting to see Connie, Saivon and me living here. "What about the neighborhood Stan?"

"It's perfect. The community is becoming more diversified. There's Hispanics, Asians, and Black folks moving in every day. Now is the time to seize the opportunity to own instead of rent," Stan said. A grimace comes over Stan's face prompting him to pause from going on further from walking. "I…have Cancer Sam," Stan said. And just like that, the conversation justifiably goes into a different direction. The news stops me in my tracks. "I indulged way too much in cigar smoking my doctor told me. I found out the hard way that whatever taste good, ain't good for you," Stan said, chuckling a bit.

"What can I do for you Stan?" Stan gathers himself with pride and places his hand on my shoulder. "I want you to take this property," Stan said. He continues showing me the house while telling me he has between six to eight months to live, and that he is going to enjoy every minute of it with his family and friends. And that's a lot of people.

Chapter 78

I bring Connie to the new home thanks to Stan. The deal is still pending, but according to Stan—it's in the bag. Saivon is with us, and just like Connie, he's wondering whose house we're entering. "Is this one of your client's house?" Connie asked.

"It could be. I'm checking it out for Insurance purposes— you know—red tape stuff." I assured her. "Check the place out Connie; give me your honest opinion on it." One person who already digs the place is Saivon. He moves about the spacious rooms like a wild cat let loose on a flock of Tweedy Birds. "Daddy, can I go and play in the backyard?!" he asked.

"Sure son, have fun alright?" Connie watches as Saivon skips outside. Connie goes over the place with a fine tooth comb, thinking she's helping me with a client.

"It's a beautiful house Sam. I'd plant a nice flower bed out front if I were the owner," she said.

"The walls could also use a paint job." I laugh as Connie is starting to rev up like a locomotive. She's letting loose that built in Interior Decorator gene that every woman has, so I figure it's time to reel her in. "So Connie, what's your overall opinion of the place?

" I'd like to give the owner an honest assessment—she's a good friend of mine," I said. Connie turned around in a whiplash movement when I mentioned that the owner was a she. "What do you mean—she?" Connie asked. I turn and walk away headed out back for Saivon. "Sam—who is she?"

"You baby." I toss the keys to Connie whose mouth is wide open.

"What do you mean—me?"

"I mean you are the owner—well we both own it," I said. I explain to Connie the details as she tries to gain her composure. "Are you sure about this?!" she asked excited. I put my arms around Connie as Saivon walks in.

"I love you Connie. If I didn't know it then, I sure know it now. I want us to be together—me, you, and Saivon." He joins in the group hug but doesn't know why, he's just a kid lovin' it man. "Do you like this house son?"

"It's cool Daddy." It's a moment straight out of a Hallmark Card. What man wouldn't want this for his family? All we need is a dog to complete the picture, and who knows, that could happen too.

I'm in good spirits since I left Connie and Saivon. I head over to see Ken before heading back to the hospital to check in on Armstrong.

Ken is being watched by Maria Ozawa, who's still a member of the police force. She promises to retire at the end of this case, but I'm not holding my breath. It's a cool fall like late afternoon, so much so that some L.A. natives are breaking out their winter gear. I bring Japanese takeout with Korean barbeque—requested by Ozawa.

I send for my man Casper to keep an eye on things so that Ozawa can catch a break. "My favorite—Korean barbeque!" said Ozawa.

She goes through the bag like a tornado hitting a trailer park. The smell itself will knock you over with cravings. "Ken, is everything cool with you?" I asked. Ken is pacing back and forth, and I believe I know why.

"How is Armstrong doing!?" asked a nervous Ken.

"The doctors think he's going to make it. Why don't you sit down and have something to eat?"

"I want to go and see him Sam," Ken demands. Ken's attachment is what I was concerned about, an assignment that goes on for some time that ends up becoming too friendly. Becoming too close to a client or vice versa, could become dangerous. "You know that's not a good idea kid," I said, breaking out a cigarette. I immediately think of Stan and his cigar smoking and Cancer. I put the cigarette out faster than a light switch going off. "There are still people out there who want to see you dead."

"But that's what I'm paying you for! I can wear a disguise or something…"

"I can fix him up Sam, I'm good at it," Ozawa intervened while wiping her mouth from the barbeque sauce. Maria makes her case for Ken, which convinces me. Hey, maybe the kid can do some good for Armstrong.

"Okay, when my friend gets here we'll go. Maria—go home and get some sleep," I insisted.

Chapter 79

Casper did arrive at the safe house, and Detective Ozawa prepared Ken exactly like she said she would. Wearing a perfect disguise, Ken is made up to look like a Caucasian youngster in makeup and hairstyle. We arrive at the hospital and enter through the loading dock entrance where the garbage is collected, and delivery trucks unload. We arrive at the room with Gary guarding like a trained Doberman. His Military training is in full display that can be overbearing to some. "Were there any problems Gary?" I asked.

"Negative Sam," Gary said. "I checked in on him all the time. No sign of hostiles." Casper smirks at Gary and his rigid demeanor.

"Take a breath General Patton—loosen up the collar a bit," he said. A little shoving ensues between the two which brings up old wounds between the two. "Fuck off Casper; you're just jealous man because you couldn't hack it!

You wanted what I got, but you chose to leave after one tour man, so deal with it." I break up the tussle between the guys as a nurse heads our way. "Listen you two; this isn't the time or the place for this old shit. I got a partner in there that needs me and now because of you two; Nurse Ratched is coming over here to shut this operation down."

"Don't worry about it Sam. Take off—I got Nurse Ratched," Casper said. Ken   and I duck inside the room as Casper heads off the nurse like a fullback blocking for a quarterback. "Nurse let me talk to you for a minute sweetness—we have some issues with the food being served to my friend in there…"

"The patient is being fed intravenously."

"That's what I mean—something's got to be done…" Casper walks the nurse down the hall, coercing the nurse with his gift for gab. Inside the room, Ken walks over to Armstrong's bedside. "Hey, Mr. Jones—it's me, Ken Yamada," Ken said. I pull up a chair alongside Ken while also keeping an eye out for Nurse Ratched. "Step aside Ken. Fuck all this Ol' Yeller shit. I know exactly what 'Strong needs." I pull out Armstrong's prized .357 silver and black

Magnum gun and place it in his large hand. "You're putting a big gun in a half dead man's hand?!" Ken asked.

"Kid, you don't understand how this man ticks. A man and his gun are like a Samurai and his sword—it's a part of him. And Armstrong is impotent without his "Sheila Baby"." We wait for a response like an audience of believers at a revival gathering after the preacher laid his hand on some poor soul's head. "I don't think this is going to work Sam," Ken said. And then it happened. First; a smile slowly gathers on Armstrong's face, followed by movement; a gentle caressing of the gun. "Hey—what if it—"

"Don't worry—it's not loaded," I assured Ken. "I think." Armstrong opens his eyes, and the first person he sees is Ken. "Who in the fuck are you?" Armstrong asked. Ken smiles at me and then Armstrong. He takes off his cap and glasses but keeps his makeup on. "It's me—Ken." Armstrong starts to remember things slowly. He looks over at me and tries to rise. "Hey, little man? Sam, get me the fuck outta' here."

"Nice to see you're back to your old self," I said. I quickly take the gun back from Armstrong knowing what was coming next. It doesn't take an Einstein to figure out he's out for blood.

He tries to rise again, but the pain is unbearable, even for him. "Who did this 'Strong?" I asked. Blood starts to seep through his wrapped bandage, caused from his moving around. "Give me back my gun, get my clothes and we can go get those bastards!" Armstrong barked.

It takes both Ken and me to hold Armstrong down as he still tries to get up. "What you gone do man, walk through the streets of Little Tokyo looking like a mummy?!" I asked. "You won't make it brotha'!" Armstrong finally lies back, exerting a lot of energy. "I hate to lose Sam!"

"I know my man. But I need you. We all need you. You tell me who it was, and me and the boys will get some payback." Casper comes in to join the group.

"Your old unit is here," Armstrong said.

"They have some big shoes to fill," I said. Armstrong conceded and spilled the beans like a star witness.

He said it was Hiroshi's crew alright, and that the leader would have killed him if not for the sirens. I leave Gary with Armstrong and I instructed Casper to take Ken back while Cleavon "the Mongol", and Buck roll with me. We're going to Little Tokyo with bad intentions in mind. It's payback for Joey and Armstrong, so there's going to be plenty of body bags needed.

Part six   The Big Payback

Chapter 80

Unbeknownst to me, Captain Pierpont has placed a new undercover cop inside Hiroshi's inner sanctum. I got a call from Detective's Thompson and Washington who has the same idea about taking out Hiroshi. They agree to meet us at a new private club that this new detective believes Hiroshi is hiding out. Sitting in the passenger seat of Cleavon's car, I look at the guys in their "moment". It's a different "moment" than I remember "in" Country when we were grunts in 'Nam.

We weren't fathers, or the head of families, dependent on drugs or alcohol, but things have changed—we're older. I drift off, daydreaming about a mission we were on; we were stationed just south of the DMZ (Demilitarized Zone) in Vietnam in the fall of '71.

We had just got back from a mission took its toll on us mentally. There was heavy casualty, especially from the South Vietnamese.

We took solace in the little time we had to go into downtown Ho Chi Minh City, Saigon for some R and R. Everybody was getting their hustle on in 'Nam man. When we weren't partying with every stripper and whore in town we were buying and selling on the black market. Drugs were everywhere. It was like Woodstock every day.

I was three months into my first tour and just like a little kid, everything seemed big to me. I had already seen my share of hell on Earth, so when we hit the town we were fired up to unleash some tension. There were at sometimes a strained relationship between us and the South Vietnamese people because of the culture clash.

Some of us shit on their sensitivities, and at times there were incidents that tested our reserve. Infiltration was rampant, causing some to lump the South in with the North. You know how it goes; they all look alike to me. My unit was a tight knit group, including some who went "off the reservation" at times.

330

There was me, Cleavon, Gary, Buck, Casper, Travis Carter Jr., Joey and Paul. We named Paul—Newman because of his blue eyes similar to the screen legend. Cleavon and Joey sometimes clashed because they were both always trying to one up each other. Casper and Travis were expert marksmen—when we needed someone to take out an enemy stronghold they were "Johnny on the spot". Travis was the only one of us to receive a medal for bravery—a Silver Star for taking out the enemy. There were relationships developed during our tours and one stood out the most among the men. A little boy named Binh who we called Benny. Benny was a great kid about the age of eleven or twelve, who always came around to sell us things.

He told us he was the main provider for his family because the father was bedridden. If he didn't work his little sister would have to be sold he said.

Benny had the trust of the men, and he would come and go with no limitations—he was like any kid you knew from your neighborhood.

On one fateful morning we were headed to town to our favorite spot but our platoon got called into action. Benny arrived and was greeted by some guys from A Company. According to one survivor, Benny had exploded in the restaurant, killing eight people. It was a shock to us all.

We later found out that an infiltrator had given Benny a special package to deliver to a First Lieutenant inside the restaurant. The poor kid was just trying to provide for his family and instead became a casualty of war. I first met Mai Nyugen shortly after that tragic incident with Benny. I saw her through the window of a noodles restaurant and had to go in and buy something. The place was mostly full with limited seating.

"Give me one bowl of noodle soup," I said, pointing at the picture. After paying the cashier, I made my way over as close to possible to Mai's table which had occupants. I was stared at because I was the only American there at the time. Here I am standing in the middle of the restaurant looking like an idiot. The seat across from Mai finally opened up and I seized it quickly.

She smiled as I must have looked desperate. It was a beautiful smile which was contagious, as the rest of the table giggled and laughed at me. All I could do was laugh at myself, and it worked. "You spilled half your soup," she said. Looking down, I realized that most of the soup was on my uniform shirt. "You speak English?" I asked, very happily

"You seem surprised. I speak three languages, including French," she said. She was like no other girl I've met there, and it showed. She was classy and smart. She told me she worked as a nurse at the Cong Hoa Hospital in Saigon, and hoped someday to be Head Nurse. We went on finding out things about each other and not realizing we had our jobs to get back to. "Can I see you again?" I asked.

"I'm here just about every day at this time," she said with a mischievous smile before exiting the place. As she left I knew, tomorrow couldn't get here soon enough. The next day came by, and Mai wasn't there, as a matter of fact she wasn't there for a whole week afterwards. After returning from another draining mission in the jungle where I was on point, I returned to that same noodle restaurant for lunch. "Let me get the Rice Noodles with fish sauce," I said.

The order taker recognized me and smiled. "You gone long time," she said. "Where you go?" Being tired and frustrated, I got a little sarcastic with her. "I go and shoot the bad guys." I'm wearing a fucking uniform!" I said to myself. I found the nearest table after accepting weeks before that I wouldn't see this woman again.

One thing is for sure is that I got accustomed to the food. In a noodle restaurant, all you hear is slurping noise. I dig in also and before I knew it, I'm slurping like a native. Suddenly standing before me is Mai with that beautiful smile of hers. She seems happy to see me. We both tried to speak first and got tangled up.

"I thought I would never see you again," I said. Mai sits down without first ordering her food. "My shift had changed, so I couldn't make it. You act as though you missed me Private Phillips," she answered. Mai is dressed in a traditional white uniform and wearing her black hair up in a ball. Her big eyes are expressive and dark, and she speaks with elegance to her that speaks volumes to her education.

"Let's just say I'm curious about you and I want to know more."

"A moth is curious about a flame also," Mai said. "There can be a danger in curiosity." We continued seeing each other as much as our duties would allow us to. Mai never expressed how she felt about me and neither did I.

I guess we both knew someday I would have to leave, so she probably felt she didn't want to get hurt. We lost contact a year later with each other as my unit came under heavy artillery fire and had to leave. I never heard from her again.

Chapter 81

Cleavon snaps his fingers in front of my face, bringing me back. "Where did you go there Sam?" he asked. "You know how it is man. I went back to the jungle," I said. "It was some good times and some bad."

"I dig where you comin' from," said Buck. Cleavon nods his head.

"Hey man—whatever happened to Carter Travis?!" he asked. "That cat was a human shooting gallery!" We all think for a moment. Carter was wound tight. Most of the snipers were. They lived an isolated existence. "I think Carter was one and done man," Buck said. "Last time I heard he was in the Midwest." I reach down and check my gun for ammo and realize I'm a little short. "Don't worry Sam, I'm the Mongol remember? My toys are in the trunk," Cleavon said.

"You guys shouldn't come, my brother. This ain't your fight." Cleavon looks over at me and shakes his head. "You were thinking about her weren't you?" he asked.

"I can't jeopardize your lives my brother." Cleavon reaches for his pack of "cigs" in his shirt pocket and pulls out a cigarette lighter and lights up. "You ever wondered why you lost contact with that girl Sam."

"I don't know; we just lost contact," I said.

"I'll bet you a fat steak dinner it was because she found out you were a part of Charlie Company. Or maybe she was catching heat for it. It was the My Lai Massacre man. Our Unit killed and raped over 400 hundred women, children, and elderly folks."

"I wasn't a part of that shit man!"

"I know brother. I was fresh off the boat, man. The Lieutenant accused those people of harboring VC. He ordered them to be gathered up and eliminated. Once the shooting started everyone else did. Some of us refused, but the Lieutenant said we'd be Court Martialed for refusing an order. I starting shooting—God forgive me. Some of the women were gang-raped or worse and to this day I can't get the screaming out of my head.

When the story got out we were called baby killers, and only the lieutenant was convicted of any crime. The Army covered up shit man because…they needed killers like me to survive that jungle and bring home the glory. After that it became easier to kill without hesitation. I figure someday those people will get their justice on all of us if not in this life—the afterlife." I can tell by the sound of Cleavon's voice that he's got tremendous regret on his shoulders. One thing is for sure; we all have some stink on us from that war. Buck reaches over and places his hand on my shoulder to comfort me and Cleavon. "At least your girl wasn't there Sam," he said.

Chapter 82

We exit off the 101 Freeway onto Alameda, in downtown Los Angeles where we look for the hot spot that Hiroshi was spotted. The streets are crowded as the residents celebrate a festival. How in the hell do we find this place with all this celebrating going on?" Buck asked. People dressed in costumes clog up traffic.

"We should have been told about this shit," Cleavon said, flipping his cigarette. We finally make it through a clearing and arrive at the location to the waiting detectives. Washington and Thompson get out of their cars to greet us.

"Charlie, Fred—how's it hangin'?" I asked.

"Like a fuckin' anvil Sam," Fred answered. Charles takes a peek inside Cleavon's car as if he was on a traffic stop.

"Who are your friends Sam?"

"You might say they're my "wrecking crew" Charlie."

"Do they know what they're up against, it can get pretty rough in there," Fred added. Cleavon smiles as he gets out of the car and head for the trunk. Buck joins him. They open up the trunk and display everything from a handgun to a grenade. Charles and Fred laugh and then quickly pull down the trunk. "You do know that the war is over, don't you boys?" Charles asked.

"You served with Sam?" Fred asked. "Charlie and I were with Bravo Company. We made it through some heavy shit brother."

"Are we through measuring our dicks? We all served our country. Now the enemy is on our turf, and he's right inside," I said. Two other cars show up that I don't recognize. Everyone reaches for their gun. "Ease up boys, it's Rico. He wanted in on the action," Charles said. "The other car looks like Ozawa's car.""What do you mean, Ozawa?!" I asked, surprised.

I had suggested that she should get some rest after watching Ken today. I guess the girl's got her second wind. "Who invited her to the party?" Fred asked.

"Maybe it's that time of the month. Ozawa always wants to shoot something when she's on the rag," Charles jokes. Rico and Maria walk up strapped to the teeth with their game faces on as though something else is cooking. "I see the gangs all here," Rico said.

"What's up Rico?" Charles asked. Rico pulls out what looks like a search warrant. I make eye contact with Maria for answers, but I get a head nod instead. "We have a man inside. His name is Fujimoto. He's going to come up next to me and order a drink, that will let you know he's a good guy," Rico said. "This is a search warrant for the premises. According to Fujimoto, The Yokohama Black Rebels are bringing in underage prostitutes in from overseas. He witnessed some brought in tonight. This underage shit will revoke Hiroshi's bail."

"We have to nail him tonight, he's a flight risk," Maria said. Rico looks at his watch as if he's waiting for something else. "Backup is late dammit!"

341

"They're probably fighting their way through traffic Rico," I said. Rico looks around and knows that timing is crucial. "Remember; wait for the agent to come up to the bar. I'll give the signal. Let's move!"

Chapter 83

We walk up to the night club as a long line of patrons are trying to get in behind the velvet rope. Several bad ass bouncers are stationed in front with clipboards and radios. It's the kind of place only a privileged few can enter. Rico, a no-nonsense Puerto Rican, leads the way past the crowd of "beautiful people" up to the door. The biggest bouncer stops Rico in his tracks. "Hold on Chico and the man. Is your name on the list?" he asked sarcastically.

"Oh, that's funny—Chico and the man—the TV show. Yes, the name is Smith and Wesson," Rico said, showing his piece. "Now get the fuck out the way." The bouncer tries to grab Rico but catches a one-two across the face sending him to the pavement. "Looo-king good Jive Turkey!" Rico steps over the man and into the club. The other bouncer gets out of the way.

Charlie and Fred show their badges to the patrons trying to get inside. "Go home people! You don't want to be here tonight!" The crowd disperses in several directions.

We enter the club to loud music of disco and funk and scantily clad Asian girls and a few other ethnicities sprinkled about. Fred shouts in my ear because of the loudness. "If I weren't on the job, I'd probably come here!" he said.

"Your wife wouldn't let you Fred," I answered back.

"Yeah—you're right!" Fred said with a hearty laugh. All of us size up the joint for the arrival of bad guys assuming we're being watched. I look up in the ceilings and spot cameras. I tap Maria on the shoulder and give her a head nod to look up. "Stay sharp Maria." There's wall to wall people that's going to make it rough on telling who the bad guys are.

Rico makes it over to the bar but immediately gets a hard stair from the bartender. Rico, tough and macho, stares right back. "Do we have a problem here?!" he asked, over the noise. The bartender looks away from Rico as a Yokohama Black Rebel member comes up beside Rico and orders a drink. His drink of choice is Vodka.

He looks over at Rico in a classic stare down. "Is that the guy?!" Maria asked. All of us wait on pins and needles for the word like a pet dog fixated on his master's fetch. Rico slams the young man in the face and then pulls out his weapon as Fred takes over the sound system. "This is the police! Anyone who is standing in this room in the next five seconds will be arrested!" Rico shouts. A mad scramble for the exits follows as I try not to get knocked down by a mob. "Where is that damn backup?!" Charles asked.

"Man, I'm the entire fucking backup you pigs need!" Cleavon boasts, pumping his shotgun. "No offense."

"None taken," Charles said. Coming out of the woodwork are the Black Rebels who are ready to rumble. Rico shows the search warrant so everyone can see. "We have a warrant to search the premises, anyone stands in the way is going down hard!" The gangsters pull out their weapons and from the look of things they have the jump on us. "Rico, they don't seem to give a fuck about your warrant," I said.

"Let's take these sucka's out man!" shouted Buck.

"Those girls have to be back there in those corridors Rico!" Charles said as a Mexican standoff has everyone twitchy. "Without backup we're fucked!" Maria added. "Hiroshi has flown the coup." A burly Japanese guy comes out with more henchmen that have us outnumbered by at least ten men. He looks like the guy that Armstrong described, and I want him. "Rico, that's the one that took out my guy."

"That fat bastard took down Armstrong?!"

"Yeah, but it took an army to do it," I said. Fujimoto, the undercover cop is still lying on the floor, whispers the name of the fat man. He said the fat man's name was Mikio alright—Hiroshi's new assassin. "Nobody touches him but me," I ordered. Mikio laughs at our small unit that's trying to bring in Hiroshi. "You have made a big mistake coming here," Mikio said in Japanese. Rico turns to Maria with a befuddled look. "Ozawa—what the fuck did he say?"

"He said you've made a big mistake coming here."

"Tell him to put his guns down or else he's a dead Jap fuck—no offense."

"None taken—this time," Maria said. She shouts at Mikio in her native tongue. He answers back with a stronger tone. Everyone starts to point a gun at each other and begin an all out shouting match. The sirens sound off in the background which gives us some much needed relief if only for a moment because I'm about to do something crazy. I point my finger at Mikio for a mano e mano battle. "Alright "Jack". Let's see how bad you are without an army to fight for you." Mikio laughs at me with my backup not too far behind. "Sam, are you crazy?" Ozawa asked me. "Don't worry—I got'em just where I want him," I assured her. I give my weapon to Cleavon and hold my hands out to show fat boy I was clean. He comes out and does the same thing. "Kick his ass Sam!" the guys said. I throw a weak punch that Mikio grabs and throws me across the room with a Judo toss. Mikio, a look-alike of "Odd Job" from "Goldfinger", picks me up and slams me on a large table. The situation is not looking good as I'm staggering about seeing two of him. "Give me the word Sam and I'll put one in his ass!" Rico said, pointing his gun. I wave him off reluctantly only because my pride wouldn't let me call it quits. Mikio talks shit to me as he stalks me for the kill. One of Mikio's men tosses a sword to him to finish me off.

"Look out Sam!" Maria shouts. I pull out a hidden gun in my ankle and put two bullets dead center in his forehead. Mikio drops back like a falling timber.

"Didn't they tell you never to bring a knife to a gunfight sucka'?" All hell breaks loose as gunfire erupts on both sides. I dive under a table and return fire. The cavalry shows up as Black Rebels begin falling like dominos. "Ozawa—you and Thompson check the rooms for the girls!" Rico ordered.

Ozawa and Thompson and the added backup rush toward the back rooms and are horrified at what they found. There are girls as young looking as twelve are huddled together in fear. The girls are mostly Asian with some Europeans as well. "We need some help in here!" shouts Ozawa. There's no sign of Hiroshi. With things falling faster than the Roman Empire, it's safe to say that he's flown the coup.

Chapter 84

I killed a man even though he was the bastard that put
Armstrong in a hospital. I have to admit that I'm not going to
lose sleep over this one. I go through the routine of making
my statement to the captain for appearances, but under the
table he's patting me on the back. Nothing is over though as
all I've done is taken out Hiroshi's enforcer, but he's on the
lamb.

Rico and the rest of the crew are outside Pierpont's door
celebrating a job well done. "I ought to take away your
license for using two crazy burnt out Vietnam Vets on this
raid Phillips, but I'll look the other way this time," Pierpont
said. "Rumor has it that Ozawa's been moonlighting for you
on occasions. Is that something I should be concerned
about?"

The captain's got me backed into a corner, and he knows it. Now it's just a matter of how he's going to use this against me. "Well…uh…she told me she could use the extra dough Captain," I answered back.

I can see the captain's mind working overtime, as he rocks back and forth on his new chair that's right out of Star Trek's Captain Kirk's. "Never mind that Phillips—it's cool man." When I hear the captain try to talk jive, I know the shit's about to hit the fan; how much shit is the question. "In light of your limited help with your man Armstrong Jones being down, I'm willing to let you keep using Ozawa—only if you can help me," Pierpont said.

"And what would that be Captain?"

"The courts you know gave that cop killer bail, and of course, he took off like a fucking jack rabbit. With our limited resources, I can use a man like you to track him down. I mean hell…you have a vested interest in bringing this killer to justice as much as we do."

"When you say limited resources Captain, how limited are we talking about?" I asked. Pierpont takes a long puff on his fat cigar before thumping the ash on the tray. "Pro bono son," he said.

The captain has said a word that I'd thought I'd never hear again. Working for free just doesn't cut it in these days of inflation. "Of course we'd give you all the support we can give…"

"You just can't give me money," I interrupted.

"I'm glad we understand each other Phillips." The survivors of the Yokohama Black Rebels are brought in and face the throng of L.A.'s finest on their way to booking. Defiant to the end, the gangsters smile as if they're under a hypnotized condition. The captain gets a good view of the punks from his big chair and is visually pissed. "In my day we'd take those thugs back in the interrogation room and show them whose town it is!" he said. "Now days they know they're rights and can quote them back to you in a New York minute."

"Captain, what if Hiroshi has slipped through the cracks and gotten out of town?" I asked.

"I don't think he's left town Sam. Hiroshi's so arrogant he's set up shop like a fat rat in your basement. We just need to send inside the right tomcat to exterminate the bastard."

351

Chapter 85

Captain Pierpont gave me a lot to think about. I'm now given full authority to bring a notorious criminal in dead or alive. Given the fact that the resources given to me is next to nothing, I know now that I need Cleavon and the gang more than ever. I head over to the "safe house" to relieve Casper while Ozawa relieves Gary at the hospital. Business is picking up.

I have a steady stream of clients that Pierpont has promised, and also some insurance and real estate clients thrown my way from Stan. If I can get the same amount of contacts that my father had I can make this thing work. I get to the "safe house" and when I put the key in the lock, the door isn't opening. I hear the sound of a pump action inside the room, so I stepped to the side of the door. "Casper—what the hell are you doing brother?!"

"Who is it?!" he shouts back.

"It's me—Sam you fool!"

"What Unit are you with?!" Casper asked loudly. I realize now that Casper is having some delusions of some sort that could prove to be dangerous for Ken. "I'm with Charlie Company soldier!" I said. "Ken, are you okay?!" Ken doesn't answer.

Casper rambles on about the invisible enemy around him. "I got the Gook tide up Captain! He got to pay for his crimes!" Casper shouts. What Casper just said makes me believe Ken is still alive. Like me and many other Vets, Casper must be on medication, and I'll bet any dollar that he's run out or forgot to take them. Knowing the house like I do, there is one way I can get inside.

I take off around the back I pry open the old lock on the door with a pocket knife and quietly walks through the house. I find Ken tied up like a stuffed pig, so I put up my finger to tell him to keep quiet. I walk him out the back out of harm's way and head back inside.

"You can't go back in there he's crazy!" said Ken.

"Ken, all of us is one pill away from ending up like Casper." I go in without a concrete plan, so I decide to be creative.

353

I know Casper loves his beer, so I grab one from the fridge and calmly walks out front to see Casper nervously pacing back and forth. Casper points the gun at me, ready to blow my head off. "Were in the fuck did you come from?!" he asked.

"It's me Casper—you asked me to come over, man. I brought your beer, just like you asked.

"I did?"

"For sho' brotha'," I said. I look over on the coffee table to see Casper's meds. Hopefully, he's still got some left. "Have a beer my brother." Casper takes the beer and while he's drinking I walk over to the table. He's still got some pills left. I convince my friend to take his meds and get him to see my "psych" doctor. Now I'm one man down in the hunt for Hiroshi until I can trust Casper again.

Chapter 86

It's my son's fifth birthday—the big one and I have to admit Connie and me went overboard in making this a special day for Saivon. We brought in some of his classmates from school along with a clown, farm animals, including small ponies to ride. At the same time, Connie is having a good time showing the parents the new house. The food is catered with a mixture of children and adult eats. We take plenty of pictures of Saivon and the other kids. Seeing the look on his face is priceless. He has just finished riding the horse, and Connie is standing next to him.

"Hold on Connie, let me take a picture with you and Saivon," I said with a big smile. "Are you having fun Saivon?"

"Yes Daddy!"

"Let me get a big smile." The look on his face is the moment that parents cherish. I get that now. I only wish that Mai could be here to see her son. "Sam, let me take a picture of you and Saivon," Connie suggested. We take more pictures—beginning a foundation to build on. My guests are beginning to arrive—people from the precinct, including Ramona, who comes over and gives me a hug in front of Connie no less. "I'm happy for you Sam. I was wrong to have said those negative things," Ramona said. "You and Constance have a good thing going—a beautiful home, a son…maybe this can happen for me someday."

"I'm sure it can, Ramona—if you want it to be," I said. Fred and Charles show up, along with the Captain Pierpont.

Between shaking hands with the detectives, I glance over to find Connie and Ramona talking and getting along with each other. Can you dig that!? A sound comes from one of Saivon's gifts that have him curious to find out what it is.

"Go ahead and open it Son!" I said. Saivon rips open the package like it was Christmas morning.

"It's a puppy!" he shouts as his friends watch. Ozawa shows up with Ken and Michelle. I calculated that they would be safe with armed police around to protect them. I made sure and told these guys that no one is to talk shop at my kid's birthday.

Some of my new neighbors come over also, bringing dishes. It's cool that they're bringing food instead of a burning cross like my father faced. "Ozawa—thanks for bringing Ken and Michelle," I said.

"No problem boss. I'm ravished. Point me to the food, Ozawa said. I pull Ken and Michelle over to the side and decide to break my own rule. Ken looks happy to be outside for a change, and I notice Michelle didn't bring Johnny. Maybe it's a good sign she dumped him after all. "How are things guys?" I asked.

"You mean after a friend of yours tried to hurt my brother?" Michelle inquired sarcastically. Ken didn't like her question as he nudges her. It seems that these two have been having noticeable disagreements for a while now, and I aim to get to the bottom of it.

I give Connie a "head signal" that only we have. Connie comes over to our little group. "Michelle, let me show you and Maria the new house," she said, gently pulling Michelle by the arm.

"I have to stay with my brother," Michelle insisted.

"I'll be okay Michelle," Ken answered back. As Connie takes the two ladies away, I need to scrape the bottom of the bowl here with Ken. "Alright Ken. I want to know why I notice you and your sister having these mini-battles against each other," I said, with a forced smile on my face. Ken suddenly has a look on his face as if he knows he and Michelle were bamboozled.

But who's really doing the bamboozling? Ken dances around my question like he was Sammy Davis Jr. "Were fine Sam. It's just a brother and sister thing—you dig?"

"Yeah kid, I dig." Just like having some of Manny's enchiladas in the pit of my stomach. Something ain't feeling right.

Chapter 87

I had wondered why my friend Stan hadn't showed up for the party at the house that he helped me get. Stan was rushed to Cedars-Sinai Medical Center and is in critical condition. Surrounded by family members Stan quietly passed away. I didn't know how sick he must have been. I sent my condolence to his wife Elizabeth and expressed to her the importance he played in my family's life. Business is a strong medicine for a sad story, so I concentrate on the main business at hand—finding Hiroshi before he finds Ken. I reopen the office for business hoping to draw Hiroshi out. This case is now a game of chess, and I've made the first move.

   Since my office is located upstairs from Miss Bernice's place, I make sure and have someone placed in the bar. I also give Miss Bernice heads up and also asked her to call me if she sees any suspicious Asian characters trying to make their way upstairs.

Miss Bernice doesn't do free though, so I promised to spy on her ex when she needs me.

Inside the office are Detective Maria Ozawa and Cleavon. Gary is with Armstrong, so that leaves me one man short, until I look up and see some good news in the form of a big, black, and bold soul brother.

"I leave on a short vacation and already you're trying to replace me!" Armstrong joked, looking weak and frail. "My main man!" I said, jumping up from my chair. I'm startled to see him, and I wouldn't be surprised to learn that he somehow escaped from the hospital. Instead, I hug him like the long lost brother he is. "How are you're feeling?!" I asked as it seems he's lost at least ten pounds. "I feel great boss—hungry, but great," he answered, looking at Ozawa and Cleavon. I know the man is weak—hell I can take him down now myself.

"Where is Gary?" I asked, not seeing the man that I put in charge of protecting Armstrong.

"You mean that stiff neck brother you had watching me? I told him that Armstrong Jones don't need a damn bodyguard man!" All I can do is laugh because I know that's who this cat is, and he's not going to change.

"So you gave him the slip?"

"You can say that. He's probably still at the hospital looking for me." Cleavon laughs, and I follow right behind him because we know that as up-tight as Gary can be, he can't stand not having control of any situation. "Armstrong, this is Cleavon. He and Gary are friends of mine from the service. They've agreed to help us out since we're undermanned.

That stiff neck brother stayed volunteered to watch over you so that those Japanese mob guys didn't finish the job with you—you dig?" The message is loud and clear. Armstrong shakes Cleavon's hand with a firm grip, showing respect to him. "I'm sorry my brother. I appreciate what you cats have done for me," he said.

"It's all good, brother. Sam has told us that you've had his back many times, so it's cool. Besides—I'd give anything to see Gary's face right now," Cleavon added. I reach in the desk drawer and pull out Armstrong's piece. "I think you'll need this," I said.

"Come to me baby! You know, somehow I felt I was holding her in my dreams." I laugh under my breath, as Armstrong is back, and that's all that matters. "I better get over to the hospital and relieve Gary and keep his honor intact. Then I'll head over to the safe house," I said.

"Let me do it boss," Armstrong eagerly responded. "I've been doing enough lying down. Me and the little man can do some catching up."

"Nice to see you back together again Armstrong," Maria said. "You had us worried for a minute there."

"Baby—they'll wish they've never fucked with me you dig?"

"They already do," Maria said. "Hiroshi's hit man was taken out by Sam." Armstrong is pissed he didn't get to meet up with Mikio himself. "Dammit Sam!"

"You're welcome 'Strong."

Chapter 88

A meeting is in play in a secluded mansion in Alhambra,
California. Some of the heads of the other factions of the
Yokohama Black Rebels are in town to discuss business. The
main topic is what's going on with Little Tokyo—mainly
Hiroshi Ito's handling of running things. No one in the room
is a day over thirty years old, but they know if they are to be
feared and respected, things have to change. It's an
unconventional meeting, as the young men are being bathed
traditional style by beautiful naked women in a gigantic
steamed bath.

Running the so-called meeting is Katashi Tanaka, a cold
blooded individual with a calm demeanor that smokes two
packs of cigarettes a day. Katashi is an opportunist who sees
that Hiroshi's misfortunes are his best chance for taking over
the top spot.

He's hosting the meeting to see who he can depend on for votes in the council. Enjoying the bath are Kei Nakamura, Juro Fukushima, Isao Sasaki, and Nobu Miyagi.

For now the men are loyal to Hiroshi. They, like Hiroshi, were tired of the way the Yakuza were running things. They believe in a more Rock and Roll style—a kick ass approach to doing things. The undisciplined approach is what has worked so far against the Yakuza so far.

"Katashi, you throw the best meetings ever!" Nobu said as he's being soaped down by two giggling girls. "I'm flattered by your compliment Nobu. Wait and see what else I have for you inside the meeting room," Katashi said.

Kei looks at Katashi with caution.

He's the oldest of the bunch and has worked for a Yakuza boss before and has the battle scar to prove it. He's missing an index finger from making his boss lose face among his peers—the result; he was "encouraged" to chop off his finger. "Katashi, is this a little foreplay before you fuck us all? Tell us why you asked us here. I'm getting bored," Kei insisted. Kei brushes away a girl's hand that's going down too far south. He pours himself a glass of champagne as Katashi laughs at Kei's embarrassment.

"You're always so serious Kei!" Katashi said. "When we were kids, you stole my bike to be accepted in your gang. My father caught you and was going to turn you in to the police, but I convinced him to let you have it because I told him that you were poor. I knew it was more important for you to have that bike than it was for me to have it. I saw the fear in your eyes Kei." Kei takes a moment to reflect on that incident and then chuckles. "I remember that!" He laughed. He finally loosens up a bit. He pours champagne on his bath girl and licks it off, to her amusement. After they were pampered in the bath, the men gather in the boardroom of the spacious mansion.

On arrival, there are two naked girls covered in food with their heads touching in opposite directions. Soft music is playing as the men eat and talk as if the women are not even there. "Very good Saki, Katashi," Nobu said. "Things must be going well for you."

"Oh, this place is just a rental. The Saki was a gift from one of the businesses we help with protection." The men nod their heads in agreement.

"You've been here now for three weeks Katashi. What have you found out about our operation?" Juro asked. Katashi picks up a sushi wrap from one girl's stomach. The next words that come from Katashi's mouth could seal the deal for their takeover of Little Tokyo, so the men calmly continue to eat and drink heartily.

"We have lost the respect of the community," Katashi uttered.

"Contact Hiroshi—we'll sit down with him," Kei said.

Chapter 89

You never keep a big man tied down for long when it comes to getting his grub on. My mother said she almost shut her place down when Armstrong paid her a visit. And her famous chicken and dumplings didn't survive round two. Armstrong is like a superhero zapped of his strength, and only soul food will bring it back. After meeting his goal for the day, I instructed Armstrong to meet me at Master Taki Akimoto's Dojo.

Master Akimoto called me and told me he'd like to help me find Hiroshi. I'm curious to know how he can. When I arrive, Armstrong is already waiting on me in the parking lot.

"How long have you been waiting here 'Strong?"

"Oh about fifteen minutes man," he said. Armstrong takes off his tie and sports coat—surprising me. "Why didn't you just wait inside big guy?" I asked.

"Master Akimoto is a scary dude man. I already had my ass kicked by a bunch of Japanese brothers. He carries that big wooden sword—he might take a swing at me with that thing, and I'd have to pull out my baby and blow his ass up."

I look at Armstrong and can't tell if he's joking or not. I guess I'd have to assume he is. "Well, we sure don't want that to happen, do we brother?" We make it inside the dojo and immediately take our shoes off in respect. I look down to see that Armstrong has holes in his socks. Master Akimoto is meditating in front of a shrine.

"I don't see any students Sam," Armstrong said as we wait. Akimoto finishes with his meditation and burns incense. "Come with me, I want to show you something," he said. We follow the master back to his office still curious as to how he can help us. "Sensei Akimoto, I appreciate you wanting to help me out, but I think we have some good people on board," I said, not wanting to embarrass him. Akimoto pulls out a photo of himself from his desk drawer dressed in uniform; a police uniform.

"I used to be a detective back in Japan," he whispered with a gravelly voice. We look at the photo in amazement. "This is you Sensei Akimoto?!" Armstrong asked.

"Yes. I was a good looking guy back then—yes?" he joked. "I was a young and optimistic cop in that photo. It was my first day on the job; Five years later I passed the detective's exam my first time." I take a quick peek in Akimoto's drawer to see awards and other photos. It seems that Akimoto was a top cop. "Why are all your accomplishments tucked away in your desk drawer Sensei?" I asked. Akimoto slowly pulls another photo out and then another.

"It's been a long time since I looked at these," he said. "I have been too ashamed to look at them over the years."

"Then why didn't you just burn them," Armstrong said.

"I still had some little pride left in me that told me I had achieved something." It seems like Akimoto is keeping something hidden inside. Everyone's got secrets—it's the type of secret it is that can cripple a person for life. "Is there something here that can help us find Hiroshi?" I asked. Akimoto pulls out a newspaper clipping written in Japanese but that shows a picture of Akimoto and another detective.

"That's me in that article, along with my partner Shinji Ishikawa. We were very close—just like brothers. We had solved a lot of cases together before we started a case that we couldn't solve—a case involving the rape and murder of schoolgirls. The killer was a sadistic bastard who was careful in not leaving any DNA. The department even asked the Yakuza for help in finding this maniac. All of the victims were shaven of pubic hairs and other atrocities.

When a politician's daughter became the tenth victim, the pressure became unbearable on Shinji and me. There was a curfew placed on the streets sending a widespread panic in the parents of little girls. Some families kept their kids at home."

"Did you make any arrests Sensei?" I asked.

"Yes. Men were brought in to save face, but I had believed that the killer was a foreigner—possibly a soldier..."

"A soldier?!" blurted Armstrong. "I guess it makes sense."
Suddenly Akimoto pounds his fists on the desk. "We brought our theory to the captain but he told us not to pursue that lead because it would cripple our relationship with the U.S.!" Akimoto snapped.

"What did you do Sensei?" I asked.

"We pursued a lead against the wishes of the department. We used a female undercover officer who wanted to help out. On two of the murders there were reports of seeing a white male in his late twenties around the areas, so we placed our undercover detective in one of the spots hoping he'd bite." Akimoto becomes a little reluctant in going further with the story. He pauses to look at a fancy Oriental designed flask that could be holding liquor. The killer became suspicious of our detective hanging around the school.

He must have spotted our car because a call was placed of an attack on another girl from another area that distracted us for a moment. The undercover officer was grabbed from right under our noses. A day later she was found brutally raped and murdered.

Shinji and I were both blamed and used as scapegoats for her death and the others.

373

We were asked to resign in shame. Shinji committed suicide three months later. My wife divorced me and took my kids." Akimoto finally grabs the flask and pours himself a drink and a cigarette. It's the sign of a man who has his own demons to conquer. I can relate to that.

"I'm sorry for your loss Sensei. Sounds like you got a raw deal," I said.

Akimoto had gone on a little longer about his case before he laid into the mind of a serial killer. He told me about the ways of Japanese social life and places that Hiroshi might be hiding. He sounded like a man who misses his old profession. Once he started talking it was like somebody turned the water faucet on full blast. "Sensei—it sounds like you want in on this operation."

"You damn right!"

Chapter 90

Katashi Tanaka is asleep in his massive bed with two young women after giving another wild party. Unbeknownst to him, Hiroshi and two of his henchmen and Hadeo are standing inside his room in the dark. The girl's mouths are covered up while they're dragged out of bed. Katashi, still drunk, rolls over with a smile on his face.

A gurgling sound awakens him to find his throat being cut. Unable to talk, the horror on his face explains it all. "Katashi, that's the sound of your throat being cut. You must have a hard time speaking. So before you die, let me do the talking for you." Katashi's eyes are popping out of his head as he tries in vain to stop the massive blood loss.

"I built this gang. Nobody is going to take what is mine. This fine house you have is all because of me. And now you're going to die in it. Sayonara old friend." Katashi dies with his eyes open. The two girls are a wreck. "What do we do with them Boss?" Hadeo asked.

"Are you girls looking for a new job?" The frightened girls nod their heads. "Well…bring them with us."

I put the word out that there's a reward for any information in helping me find Hiroshi. The store and business owners weren't particularly fond of Hiroshi anyhow, so I passed out my business cards. One owner who didn't take too kindly to us was the owner of an exotic goods store. It specializes in novelties and jewelry for tourists.

"You're a police officer?" he asked.

"No, I'm a Private Investigator. My name is Sam Phillips. Here's my card." The owner takes my card and looks at it up and down before he crumbles it up and tosses it in the garbage. "Now that's not very nice. I paid a lot of money to have those cards made." Armstrong pulls out a gold cardholder and hands the man his card. Armstrong's menacing stare forces the store owner to think twice about throwing his card away.

"When did you have cards made?" I asked.

"Hey brotha', I'm a P.I. now. I want to be ready when my license comes in you dig?"

Armstrong said, feeling proud of himself. "Why are you looking for Mr. Ito? He's given money back to the community," the owner said.

"He's also responsible for multiple murders in the community," I pointed out. "He's also brought drugs and prostitution here also. You're paying him protection money also. But it's extortion for them not to come in here and smash your place up isn't it?"

"You don't understand Japanese culture," the owner insisted.

"Make me understand my friend. Hiroshi Ito killed a store owner like you for trying to help the law. He destroyed the Yakuza competition in town, and he's killed police officers. He's a bad man sir. Help me get him off the street." The store owner looks around outside for precautions. It's a good sign so far. Most of the others have given us the twenty-second rule. "Give me your card again," he said. Progress begins when you put a crack in a concrete wall. Armstrong and I just did that.

Chapter 91

We meet up with Sensei Akimoto outside a noodle restaurant following up on a lead of his. It's the first time I've seen Akimoto outside the dojo, and the first time without his gi on. He looks refreshed in a way—almost as if he wants to return to police work. He jumps in the car with us in the backseat. "Did you bring us some steamed noodles?" Armstrong asked with a straight face. "Don't mind him Sensei, he's always hungry. What's shaking?"

"The delivery man inside is a student of mines," Akimoto said. "He told me that Hiroshi Ito always orders from this noodle restaurant at eight tonight. We could follow my student to Hiroshi's place tonight…"

"Wait a minute Sensei, helping us to find Hiroshi is one thing, but helping us bring him down is another," I said. "I can't have another person I care about get hurt. This battle is personal between Hiroshi and me." Akimoto makes his case as to why he should come with us.

We go inside the restaurant to eat after all to fill our bellies and to talk with Akimoto's student, but only for a brief moment. We leave a good tip on the table to sway any curious notions about us. Later on I bring in my army buddies who want a piece of Hiroshi themselves, including Casper, who returns from a stint in the Looney bin. Gary walks into the office with a room full of guns pointing at his face. With Hiroshi still on the loose, a man just can't be too careful.

"Okay guys, it's me. You can lower your guns now," Gary said.

"How do we know you weren't invaded by a body snatcher, brother?" Buck asked. I can't tell if Buck is joking or if he seriously believes that. "Alright guys, let's stay together here.

We have some serious shit to do tonight," I insisted. Everyone settles in as we wait for Akimoto. I look at my ragtag unit and can clearly see they are definitely not the "Untouchables", but I know each one of these men and Ozawa too would have my back in a dark alley. If anything, they are more like "The Wild Bunch". But those cats and

"The Magnificent Seven" went out in a blazing glory. My goal is to come out alive to be able to watch my son grow.

We hear footsteps again coming down the hall. This time I make sure the guys lower their guns. The door opens and its Akimoto with his student, a fresh faced Asian teen with mother's milk still on his breath. Akimoto and the kid get a lukewarm reception from Cleavon and the guys. "Nice of you to join us Sensei Akimoto," Armstrong said. Cleavon and the boys view Akimoto as just another yellow man. "He looks just like the guy we're chasing," Buck stupidly said. I shake my head knowing this is not going to end well for Buck.

"How do we know he won't lead us into a trap?" Buck looks down on Akimoto with distrust. Akimoto tries to avoid confrontation like a true warrior does, but he's joining a pack wolves fighting for pecking order. "This is my student— Ryota. He's delivered food to Hiroshi for weeks now. Tonight when Ryota makes his deliveries we will be there to follow him." Cleavon stands up from my couch to confront Akimoto now. Armstrong just shakes his head. "What do you mean "we" old man? You haven't proven a damn thing to this mission. You want to join our foxhole you have to show us you won't book when the shootin' starts."

Cleavon makes a move on Akimoto and pays for it with a throw down, and his face pinned down on my dirty floor. "Okay—he's cool!" Cleavon whispered.

Chapter 92

We loaded up two vehicles after our meeting in my office and headed straight for the 101 Freeway. Cleavon is still suffering from the beat down he took from Akimoto. The look on his face is more of embarrassment than anything else. "Are you okay "Mongol"? I asked with a smirk on my face. "I guess we forgot to tell you that Akimoto is a master of martial arts." Armstrong, sitting in the back seat, burst out laughing as only he could. "Man—you got your ass whupped! He was slamming your ass around like a cartoon character!"

Cleavon pulls out a gun and points it at Armstrong. Armstrong's laugh takes a serious turn. "Sam, I know this burnt out cat is a friend of yours, but if he don't take that gun out my face I'm going to stuff it so far down his throat it's going to come out through his ass."

"Cleavon—what the fuck are you doing man?" I asked with nervous calm.

"I'm going to need both you brothers alright? That shit was funny inside the office. Get over it! Armstrong didn't mean anything by it, did you 'Strong?" Armstrong is not one for taking one for the team, but he is a man that's one more offense from doing some serious time in prison. "Everything is groovy man." Cleavon slowly turns around and pockets his gun. Armstrong puts away his baby that I didn't know he had pointed at the back seat of Cleavon. Watching over my army buddies is as dangerous as watching over kids playing with C4 Dynamite. The brothers are wound pretty tight.

A reclusive Hiroshi is on the phone surrounded by his trusted men. He's living in a rented mansion, unlike his last pad. The place is set up in a way that the men could drop everything when need be. Hiroshi is on the phone talking with someone while Hadeo and two men play cards. Whoever is on the phone is putting a big smile on Hiroshi's face.

"I'm glad you've come to me. I'm a peaceful man, and can be a trusted ally when you need me. Hiroshi points to Hadeo to get his attention. "You won't be sorry." He hangs up the phone.

"Get ready. We have a job to do!" Hiroshi said.

"What about the food?" Hadeo asked.

"It can wait." Hadeo and his men drop the cards with curious looks on their faces. "A gift was just handed to us." The men put on their cool jackets and head for the door. As the door opens, Ryota is standing there with the food. Hiroshi sees two cars pull up behind Ryota's car and panics. "It's a trap. Hadeo grabs Ryota and make a run for the car. Gary and Casper take shots at Hiroshi and Hadeo.

"What are your men doing Sam—they'll kill Ryota?!" Akimoto shouts.

"They're going off the reservation Sensei!" I shouted back. Hiroshi fires back with a sinister smile on his face as they speed off. I pull up next to Gary on the passenger side as he reloads his gun. "Did you not see Ryota being taken hostage Gary?" I asked calmly.

"Hey man—the kid's collateral damage. He had a target on his back as soon as you and the old man got him involved! Now do you want this guy Hiroshi or not?!" In a way, the crazy bastard made sense. We got Ryota involved, and I signed off on it. "He's getting away Sam. You want to move your ass?"

"I want to make this clear in a language you and Casper will understand Gary. I'm the fucking platoon leader on this mission you got that? You pull that John Wayne shit again I'll ship your asses back to whatever rock you crawled from under. You can take that to the bank—brother." I speed off— flooring the Riviera like a bat out of Hell.

After about a mile I finally see Hiroshi's car up ahead weaving in and out of traffic. "Stay on 'em Sam!" Armstrong yells. I get close enough to see Ryota struggling to get free in the back seat. Hiroshi's car swerves and rams into a car, sending the other car spinning out of control. "He's headed for the freeway!" Akimoto shouts.

"If he gets to the freeway—we have no shot Sam!" Cleavon said.

"Get closer…closer! Akimoto pleads. The passenger back door opens.

"What the fuck is he doing?!" I asked. My question is answered horribly as Ryota is tossed out the car.

"Oh my God," Armstrong shouted. I swerve to avoid the kid, but to our horror, Ryota is struck and killed by Buck. We screech to a stop as Hiroshi gets away. Akimoto is stunned and speechless. "Sam, we can't let the fuzz know those dudes are your friends. That'll be the end of us," Armstrong whispered.

"Quick—you and Cleavon get their guns before the circus starts. I rush up to what's left of Ryota with Akimoto a crumpled mess. Armstrong and Cleavon do their thing as witnesses come out of the woodwork. "You brothers be cool. It was an accident so play it out. Give us your pieces. Remember—everyone seen those cats throw that poor kid out the door—dig? Armstrong asked.

"Yeah man. Solid." Gary replied. We handle the police like a fine violin, as the few witnesses that did see what happened told the same thing we mentioned to police. But a kid I hardly knew is dead, leaving Akimoto to tell the family the bad news. Again, Hiroshi evades me and the law while racking up dead bodies all over town.

A grieving Akimoto watches as Ryota's body is covered up. Armstrong pulls me to the side for a one on one. "I got a bad feeling Sam. This Hiroshi is a ghost. He looked like they were on their way out when Ryota came to the door. We've got no leads—just dead friends."

"What do you suggest we do 'Strong?" I asked.

"We have to go back to the way we did things in the past, you and me. Babysitting your old unit is not a road I'd like to go down anymore," Armstrong said.

Chapter 93

Ozawa and Ken are watching television on an uneventful evening. The living room could use a maid or two as Ozawa watches Ken again look at his watch. On the table in front of them is an ashtray full of used up cigarette butts the two have smoked. "You're going to burn a hole in that watch of yours kid," Ozawa said. Ken gets up from the sofa and softly paces.

"I was wondering if you can go on a delivery run."

"What you have in mind?" Ozawa asked.

"I have a taste for Kentucky Fried Chicken, mash potatoes with gravy, and beer."

"You get one beer. And when I get back you better have this place clean before the boss gets here. Ozawa stretches her stiff legs from hours of sitting. "I bet you're looking forward to going home, huh Ken?" Ozawa said, putting on a lightweight jacket. Ken seems disinterested and preoccupied in his thoughts. This place is home—I was born here."

"Oh, I forgot that." Ozawa leaves, not before telling Ken to lock the door behind him.

When Ozawa is out of sight, Ken shuts the door but doesn't lock it. He's expecting someone. He's like a teenager on a hot date with the most popular girl in school kind of nervous. He sits and waits. The doorknob turns. To his horror, it's Hiroshi and his men.

"What are you doing here?! Where is Michelle?!" Ken asked defiantly. Hiroshi and his men laugh.

"She sends her regards. She sent us instead," Hiroshi said. "You have caused me a lot of trouble Ken Yamada.

"Wait—I'm not who you think I am."

"You're exactly who I think you are. And now you're going to tell me everything about Sam Phillips." Hadeo walks over to Ken and slugs him in the stomach. He's then pounded continuously until he gets the message. "I want to know all about this man's family!" Hiroshi motions for his henchmen to take Ken with them. Hiroshi stands and looks around the safe house. "Checkmate Mister Phillips."

Ozawa returns to find the safe house door partially open. She drops the food and pulls her weapon. Cautiously, she walks in, peeking around corners quickly. She notices blood splatters on the floor and becomes concerned.

With her gun, raised she continues through the house. "Ken!" Getting no response, she puts in a call to Sam.

After getting the call from Ozawa, I immediately contacted Armstrong with a gigantic reluctance knowing how attached he was to the kid. His personal attachment is what Armstrong will have to learn not to do, being a good Private Dick. "What happened here Maria?" I asked.

"I went out for food because the kid asked me for Kentucky Fried Chicken," she said as Armstrong bravely keeps it together. "I told him to lock the door behind me, but when I returned, I noticed the door partially opened." I look over at the door that even a rookie cop could tell it wasn't broken into. He was expecting someone Maria. The door wasn't busted through." Maria shakes her head pissed off.

"What's up?" I asked her.

"I think Ken was trying to get rid of me—the way he kept looking at his watch and acting funny."

"This whole case has been funny. Those two have been acting weird since the day they walked into my office. The last few weeks I've seen them arguing with each other," I said.

"Sam. Ken was expecting his sister Michelle to come through that door."

"She sold him out to Hiroshi. They're not sister and brother. And I was the longhead sucker that fell for a scam. Michelle, you call Pierpont—"

"It hasn't been twenty four hours…"

"He'll want to know! Let's go 'Strong!"

Chapter 94

We drive up and down the streets of Little Tokyo looking for any traces of activity. I unleashed Armstrong again on the community to do what he does best—shaking down the weaklings who might have seen something. "Somebody better tell me something here or I'm gonna' do a sequel mutha'...!"

"We don't know anything!" one man said.

"Where is Hiroshi?! He took a little friend of mine! A Japanese kid trying to make a better life for himself, but you protect that monster!" It went on like that for two hours with no success. Things are more tightened around here than a chastity belt. And that ain't cool.

With the sun coming up soon and being no closer to finding Ken, we left Little Tokyo the way we found it—a town known for keeping dark secrets. As we drive towards the "safe house", I receive a call on my car phone. "Sam Phillips P.I., make your case." It was disturbing what I heard next. I look over at Armstrong, and he could tell what was coming next.

I hang up the phone and make a U-Turn on Wilshire Boulevard. "They found Ken. He's dead." Armstrong lowers his head in pain. We both got to know the kid even though we got duped. "Sam, somebody's got to pay." I know that look. It's like the look Bruce Lee had when he found out someone killed his teacher in "The Chinese Connection".

We make it to the crime scene in the downtown industrial park area. Ken is being pulled from a large trash bin. Captain Pierpont is there too. For him being here at a crime scene so early in the morning is not a good sign—for me. "Look what they done to the little guy," said Armstrong. His body is mutilated with fingers missing with large chunks of flesh also. "He was tortured Captain," the coroner said.

"Whatever these bastards wanted he put up one hell of a fight." The captain has me in his crosshairs and makes a beeline for me and Armstrong.

"Is this your boy Sam?!" Pierpont asked.

"That's Ken alright Captain."

"That's two people dead around you in less than twenty-four hours Sam. I told you to bring this kid in. He'd probably still be alive." Armstrong takes a run at Pierpont, but I restrained him. Several policemen get in between us before anything transpired.

"You want to lose your license before you've become a P.I. brother?!" I whispered strongly in Armstrong's ear. "This is how the game is played dealing with the law."

"He's a racist pig man!" Armstrong said.

"That racist pig will throw a bone your way when the cases are not coming fast enough. Now chill man!" Armstrong walks away to cool down. Pierpont walks back over I guess to keep biting me in the ass like a bulldog. The best way to describe Pierpont's demeanor right now is to think of Sgt. Carter of "Gomer Pyle" on cocaine. The dude's all over the place. "You keep that big bear in check Phillips or he's back in the slammer you got that?"

The captain's tone has toned down. Now either the man's mellowing in his old age or the jive turkey's about to lie something on real thick—the bullshit. "Armstrong's cool Captain. He's new to the game."

"I put you on this case to see what you were made of Sam. Your father—God rest his soul would have caught this bastard by now," Pierpont said. "If you can't handle the job I can get my boys to go in the cleanup spot for you. But you'll never get another case from me."

"Is this how you played my father Captain? I don't need to jump through hoops man! Remember—this mother fucker took out two of your finest, so don't play that shit with me! You ain't Frank Sinatra, and I'm sure not Sammy Davis Jr. you dig. Give me 48 hours, and I'll bring him in dead or alive."

"Dead will do just fine Sam. I'm glad we've had this talk."

"Later, man."

Part Seven the Bushido Way

Chapter 95

The Bushido Code is what Akimoto practiced. According to Ken's explanation of the Bushido Way, in Samurai days, Akimoto would have committed Seppuku—"ritual suicide" for the handling of his case in Japan. With the killing of Ryota, I sensed a blank look in his eyes.

The Bushido Code also speaks of philosophy on revenge. It's best served cold. I remember the code, and so does Armstrong. I drop the big guy off at the office to pick up his car. We were still reeling from Ken's death. He made not have been the real Ken, but the kid had a lust for life, and he didn't deserve to go out with the morning garbage.

Armstrong and I were thinking the same thing, and it wasn't pretty. "Meet me back here at eight tonight," I said. Armstrong gives me a head nod and we part ways.

I went home to be with my family in what seemed like an eternity since I've seen them With Saivon in school I sat

Connie down and told her the news about Ken. Connie has a shocked look on her face but handles it fairly well. "So, Ken or whoever he was, was not the real Ken Yamada?" she asked. "We were bamboozled Connie.

My decision to take this case has had a domino effect that's caused people's lives." Connie gives me a big hug— the kind your grandmother would give after telling you everything is going to be alright.

"Why don't we take a vacation Sam? We can drive up the coast to Napa Valley. I heard it's beautiful up there this time of year."

"Private Investigators don't take vacations. Who's heard of such a thing?" Connie can see the reaction I had on my face, but it doesn't stop her. "It will be a good chance to bond with your son," she said—bringing out the big guns. "You make a good point "foxy lady". Getting away for a few days doesn't sound too bad at all," I said with a sly smile. "I could hand over my cases to Armstrong or maybe Cleavon…

"Okay…if you unleash those two guys on any of your cases, you won't have a business to come back to."

We both laugh at that scary thought. Armstrong is not ready to be on his own, and Cleavon will receive his pink slip and severance pay soon. Like Armstrong said, if we want to lose our licenses fast, just keep my army buddies on the payroll.

"After this case, we'll take that vacation, as a family," I said. Connie's beautiful face lights up like the sun after a rain shower. She wraps her arms around my neck and plants a big kiss on my lips. "Now that's the man I fell in love with."

Word gets around about the murder of Ken to all my friends and associates. As I walk in Miss Bernice's place, I get the walk of shame look from everyone as I pass through. Hell, even Miss Bernice is showing a little civility my way. "I let your army buddies upstairs just like you asked me Sam. Afterwards, you come down and have a drink like old times," she said, in a not so boisterous tone I've been used to. "Can I get a rain check Miss Bernice, I have to go back out tonight—I need my head clear."

"Alright, you hang loose Sam. Remember, if you need some help, my old man used to be a stone cold killer in the war." It's just what I need, another killer from the war. All of us are fucked up from it and on some drug we're popping like jelly beans.

Chapter 96

Akimoto is kneeling and meditating in front of a Buddha statue. Next to him is a prized Samurai sword. Ozawa walks in unannounced. She lets Akimoto finish his meditation. "I can feel your presence Maria. I know why you're here," Akimoto said. Maria notices the sword beside Akimoto instead of the wooden one. "I see you have your prized sword with you," she said. Akimoto stands up and with the sword in his hand. His dojo's prized possessions have been taken down from the walls.

Maria kicks her shoes off and comes all the way inside. "I heard about Ryota Sensei. And I know what you're about to do."

"Then you know it's pointless in telling me not to do what I'm about to do. It's the Bushido Code."

"I too have suffered a loss last night," Maria said. "Let us handle Hiroshi."

"I tried it your way, and Ryota paid the price. I brought shame to his family and myself. Hiroshi is evil, and must be stopped, or the community will fell to prosper." Maria goes in front of the Buddha statue and lights an incense stick. "Then I will come with you—and you will not stop me," Maria insisted. She kneels and begins to meditate.

"You have not lived yet Maria, but you're prepared to die. You have never thought about starting a family someday?" Akimoto asked.

"If I had a family this would be harder to do," she responded. Akimoto becomes suddenly proud of Maria. He kneels down beside her. "I'll say a prayer for the both of us."

When I arrived in the office, the guys were helping themselves to my liquor and cigars, and it's not even "Happy Hour". The cigars are used only when I close a case, and as far as I know, this case ain't closed. The guys have now become that loser relative you can't get rid of, which now makes my decision easier. "What's up boss?!" asked Glen, sitting on my desk.

I sit down at the desk and open up my drawer to pull out the checks. "Are you guys enjoying yourselves?" I asked. Cleavon holds my Remy Martin bottle up in the air—like he bought it. "Man, we were celebrating the Olympic Boxing team getting the gold. That young cat Sugar Ray Leonard is going to be a champ someday!" I haven't paid close attention to the Olympics for obvious reasons. "If you haven't noticed Cleavon, I've been busy on a major case involving people I know getting killed around me. So forgive me if I'm not up on current events!" The guys are taken aback from my reaction. "Whoa Sam," Cleavon said. "We're sorry for what happened out there last night too. But life goes on brother."

"I'm glad you said that brother. Life does go on. And I'm going on without you brothers. Your services are no longer needed," I said, handing out the checks. "I put a nice bonus in there for you all for coming to my aid. The heat I'm catching from the captain is too intense to keep you on." Each one of the guys opens their envelopes to see an extra fifty dollars in hard cash.

"Hey, this is groovy Sam!" Buck rants. "I can respect your decision brother. Hell—I knew this wasn't going to be permanent." Gary folds his envelope after he pockets the cash.

"It's been real Sam. Having the unit back together was special—just like old times." We slap five on it and hug it out. "You got a good thing going here my brother," he added

"Thanks, Gary. You give them sucka's hell man." That's how it went for the next twenty minutes or so. I calmed down and realized these bad ass dudes were a part of my life for two tours—and saved my ass on more than one occasion. The least I can do is send them off proper.

Chapter 97

I'm out of work again, but that's the kind of year it's been. I fought to get the case of the murder of actor Sal Mineo in West Hollywood. The hunt was on for the killer, but being that it was a high profile case, the powers that be passed on having a Black man being questioned by the press. That's my unofficial version of what happened.

It's the year of "Rocky" and Taxi Driver at the movies, and Cleavon was right…the Summer Olympics was owned by Bruce Jenner, Nadia Comaneci, and the boxing team with the Spinks boys, and Sugar Ray Leonard. Jimmy Carter is the new president. He has a big job in front of him, but at least he got my vote.

I received a call earlier out the blue from Lauren Tolliver—out of the hospital since her daughter Sidney shot her. It's not every day that your own daughter tries to kill you. As I pull into the driveway of her mansion, I remember what it was like back two months ago. It seems like a lot longer. All hell had broken loose, with the driveway full of grimy photographers and reporters trying to make a fast buck on a famous actress's misery.

A sad looking Sidney stared at me with that distant glaze—whispering incoherently. It's the type of scandal that became synonymous with the way Hollywood functions.

A familiar face greets me at entrance to the front of the house. Harold steps out to greet me with a look on his face that catches me off guard. He seems to be happy to see me, or maybe I had too much to drink earlier. "Mr. Phillips is so good to see you sir," Harold said. I pinched myself to see if I still had Black skin and an underpaid and underappreciated job.

"It's nice to see you too Harold, my man." Harold even opens the door for me, something he never did before. If he gets any nicer, I'm going to owe him lunch. "A lot of Mrs. Tolliver's friends have stopped coming around…

you know…since the incident," Harold said. "This community can be kind of ruthless sir. They're not friends—just mere acquaintances living the same privileged lifestyle." From the way Harold's talking, it seems like Mrs. Tolliver's been blacklisted. Mrs. Tolliver is becoming this year's version of Gloria Swanson from "Sunset Boulevard". Each year a famous actress is put out to pasture just for getting past the age of 40. Maybe Marilyn saw the writing on the wall. I just don't want to become the William Holden character from the movie—he died you know. "I dig where you're coming from Harold. Where is Mrs. Tolliver?" I asked. "This way sir," replied Harold. Harold leads me through the massive home that felt like walking through a maze. However, the place seems empty.

I look to my left up the staircase—looking for Sidney to come walking down the stairs with that seductive smile of hers. But it was not to be, as reality jolts me back into place. We take a short detour from the usual place I was taken to visit Lauren.

"Are we not going to the den Harold?" I asked with curiosity.

"No sir. Mrs. Tolliver is in the theater room," he said. The theater room, I thought to myself. It's a place where legends go to die. Harold opens the door and guides me in a dimly lit small theater that's bigger than most theaters I've been to in the city. On the screen is Lauren in her younger days playing in what looks like an Italian epic period movie.

Usually, when an American actor goes to Italy to do a movie, it's to save their career—so I was told. Lauren is sitting quietly—examining her performance. In one hand is a glass I suspect is not water, and in the other is a cigarette. Harold walks between the seats to get the starlet's attention.

"Ma'am—Sam Phillips is here to see you," Harold announced. He makes his way back over to me, waiting outside the aisle.

"She'll see you now sir. She's in a delicate place right now. Please take that into consideration."

"You have my word Harold." Harold leaves not before glancing back at Lauren like a star crossed lover or broken hearted fan. "Come in Sam. It's nice to see you again," Lauren said. "Look at me up there. Wasn't I beautiful then?"

"A man would have to be blind not to know that you were a fox Mrs. Tolliver—and still is," I reassured her. Lauren smiles while not taking her eyes off herself. She's still a stunner today—paying for all the beauty money can buy. "That movie is called Hercules—Son of Zeus," she said. The director couldn't keep his hands off me on that production." The look in Lauren's eyes tells a thousand stories. She revels in each moment of the scenes—reliving them in her mind. I look at my watch and notice that nighttime is approaching fast and that I still have one more stop to make before calling it a night.

"You did call me here for a reason—right Mrs. Tolliver?" I asked politely.

"Life was so much simpler then Sam."

"I guess it depends on who you're talking to ma'am," I replied directly. She looks over at me and notices what I meant. "I guess I never thought of it that way," she said. "Come with me Sam, I have something to show you." Lauren leads me into the den from a different entrance point of the house. Once inside, everything starts looking familiar again. "I just had to go out and pick up more pieces," she boasted.

Lauren is still moving her lips and saying nothing as I monitor my watch. Then she makes a beeline to her locked vault. She pulls out something that must be of value— otherwise why keep it there. "You want to see something beautiful?" she asked. Lauren pulls open a small pouch from a case. She opens the pouch and pulls out a green diamond shaped necklace.

"My Emerald stone is back where it belongs."

"What did it do, find its way home like Lassie?" I asked sarcastically.

"It showed up in a package with no return address. Isn't that odd?" Convenient," I said to myself. If someone stole it why would they return it and risk getting caught?

"Yes, it's very odd. I guess now you have everything you wanted. I guess that's it." Since I never have seen the stone up close and personal, I am curious a little what a stone that men would kill for looks like.

"May I see the stone Lauren? It's not every day a man of my means comes across such a treasure."

"But of course Sam." Lauren hands over the emerald necklace that fits in my hand almost like a baseball would. "I'm going to have diamonds added to it next. That will increase the value," Lauren said. It'll increase the value and the danger element. "It's a beautiful piece Lauren. Don't you think you should put it somewhere more…fitting?" Lauren pretends she didn't hear my suggestion. She heads over to her desk and pulls out a checkbook. Over my shoulder is a painting of her husband. She looks up at him as she prepares to write.

"I'd like to pay you for your handling of the case Sam," she said.

"But I didn't find your necklace—you did. We're all square."

"Nonsense," she replied. "If it weren't for my daughter and her loser boyfriend, you would have found it I'm sure. Will five thousand be sufficient Sam?"

Inside, my body is doing "The James Brown", but my head is telling me not to jump back and kiss myself just yet. "I'm feeling there's more to this generous payout that it just being the kindness of your heart Lauren," I said. Lauren finishes writing. She tears the check from her book and holds it out. "You're a smart man Sam, and a fine investigator. I could have used you more in the past," she said. "My daughter is going to be reaching out to you to testify at her trial if it goes to that. I would like you to testify for me instead."

"It looks to me that I'm being sucked into a war between you and your daughter all again Lauren." Lauren smiles, thinking she has me by the balls. Any other day I'd might just play that torture game. "Lauren, I think you're trying to buy me off."

413

"Isn't that part of your job Sam?" she asked. "My daughter can't afford to pay you this kind of money. If you won't take money, what would you take?" Lauren slowly opens her blouse and puts the check inside. She walks over to me and wraps her arms around my neck.

"We could take this to another level if you like."

I look down Lauren's blouse not particularly knowing if I'm interested in the check or the breasts she's offering up so politely. "It's a dangerous game you're playing Mrs. Tolliver. A black widow spider comes to mind. If I get trapped in your web, I will be in a state of euphoria for ten minutes—up until you bite my head off."

I pull Lauren's arms off in fear of a sting. Lauren turns around—her back towards me in what seems to be a feeling of embarrassment. "I'm sorry Sam. I don't know what came over me. Everyone has turned away from me including Hollywood, my daughter, also you to a point. Can you forgive me?"

"There's nothing to forgive Lauren. It's Hollywood's loss. A fox like you not being on screen is criminal. You have the money baby.

www.ingramcontent.com/pod-product-compliance
Lightning Source LLC
Chambersburg PA
CBHW030348030726
47497CB00002B/231